July 2015

To Chris

Fury

FACT AND FICTION WROTE BY DON FLEMING
WITH STRONG LANGUAGE AND VIOLENCE

Best Wishes and all The Very Best

Don Fleming

authorHOUSE®

AuthorHouse™ UK Ltd.
500 Avebury Boulevard
Central Milton Keynes, MK9 2BE
www.authorhouse.co.uk
Phone: 08001974150

© 2009 Don Fleming. All rights reserved.

No part of this book may be reproduced, stored in a retrieval system, or transmitted by any means without the written permission of the author.

First published by AuthorHouse 11/19/2009

ISBN: 978-1-4490-2380-5 (sc)

This book is printed on acid-free paper.

What a change from the past to the present day from playing with marbles and street games to joy riders to burglary, muggings, rape and murder.

Once upon a time you could leave your door unlocked and not be afraid, now you need locks upon locks, alarmed and if you can afford it, CCTV cameras and still worry, worry because they are there, the head bangers who just don't care they will still do what they want to do no matter what, to cause havoc.

There have been pickpockets and petty thieves since time began, but not the scale it is this modern present day, there is little respect for anything or anyone not even the police, why? , Ask yourselves why, ask the do-gooders about human rights, the only people that demand human rights is the guilty, does anyone think that a person who is about to be raped, killed, or beaten up and asked these scum for human rights! do you think they would listen!?, you can ask them that yourself, ask the politicians?, ask them why?, ask the judges why?, why muggers, rapists, burglars, paedophiles , thieves and murderers get away with these things so lightly!, they would say corporal punishment is inhumane, would hanging a murderer also be inhumane?, they have legal rights!, human rights!, what about the change of lives that these people do to the innocent!, that is inhumane!, the way the law is it protects the guilty, the not guilty have to protect themselves!, when one says protect one self! It means if you are attacked by another party or parties you will have to prove you reacted the right way, you will have to prove you did this in self-defence! Otherwise the guilty parties if they are injured they could sue for injury, you have to protect your home and personal possessions the best way you can with what you can afford, of course some people have a pet dog and hope that will keep unwanted visitors away.

There was an incident when an intruder went into a widows bungalow in the early hours of the morning she had such a pet usually a very placid Labrador, but the dog attacked an intruder and bit his hand and went straight through the intruders leather glove, then the dog went for the persons leg, grabs the intruders trousers then grabs again and bites the persons leg, at this time the man is very scared and starts shouting at the dog! " get off you bastard !" , the same time the old lady! Mary Benson a smallish grey haired plumpish lady came through into the living room turned the lights on and shocked what she saw! Immediately went to the phone and rang the emergency service, requiring both ambulance and police, the services was quick to reply and was at Mrs Benson's in just a few minutes! With the dog stood near the intruder! The medics that came in! Checked the intruder for damage to himself what the dog had done to him! Then was taken to hospital with one of the two policemen that came following the ambulance! While the other officer took particulars from Mary, but the only thing that Mary could tell the officer was what she saw when she opened the door when she went into the room! She said she saw sandy her beloved Labrador shaking the mans leg! Who was on the floor shouting the French windows open and an overturned coffee table! She said she was woken by a noise from the room and sandy barking, the other officer that followed the ambulance, and after the man had been attended to by the hospital staff! In the mans statement to the officer by saying! He was passing the bungalow when he looked and saw what looked like a torch light in the bungalow, he went to investigate, and entering through the open French doors, someone rushed by him! Then the dog attacked him, he was asked! Why he was out so early in the morning? He replied by saying he could not sleep, so he went for a walk, the officer asked? " Do you always wear gloves on a warmish night? " the man replied by saying he wears gloves a lot you just don't know how the weather is going to be! Asked by the officer? If the torch was his! Near the turned over coffee table he said no replying that probably the intruder dropped it! Who I nearly caught, if the dog hadn't have attacked me, asked by the officer? " Why do you think the dog never attacked the intruder before you came? " he said, " I don't know, ask the bloody dog? Maybe he was asleep? maybe he knew the person? I don't know, I don't fucking care now! All I do know is that if I see anything suspicious again, ill turn the other way".

The man treated at the hospital, and then later sued Mrs Benson for injuries caused by her dog! .

He was a man with no police record, he received compensation there was no evidence to say that what he said, was not the truth! Nothing was taken from the property, no one was ever found for this intrusion! Although an attack by an animal that is found to be a dangerous animal, would be by law have to be put down, but by evidence given from people such as the postman, milkman and other callers saying that sandy was a lovable friendly dog and the court taking into consideration it was dark and the scent of a person he did not recognise in his home! It is good to say sandy is still at home with Mary.

What seems to be strange about this incident is what was sandy doing when the intruder broke in? Was he in a deep sleep at first? Did he know the so-called intruder? We possibly will never know. That was a mild burglary incident.

Things will get worse until the fury of the right comes out! Right is right, and wrong is wrong, the punishment to fit the crime, and an eye for an eye, and a tooth for a tooth, but don't take the law into your own hands. Police is the law and parliament make the laws, but who's side is the law on?.

This story is about another widow, a younger slim widow of 58, a very attractive 58 year old lady with lovely long blonde hair and a figure to fit it, who had suffered losing her husband three years ago, he was a very tall fair haired sixty year old, who suffered a heart attack that was fatal, and later herself having a bad stroke leaving her paralysed down one side of her body, leg and part of her neck! Her speech came back to her, she spends most of her time in a wheelchair, her name is Jean Longhurst and she lives in a nice semi, with her son Johnny! Who is a detective sergeant in the local police who is tall like his father and the good looks of his mother he's 39 yrs of age, Jean has another son Frankie named after his father a more rugged looking man tall like his dad and the looks of his father, a 32 year old, he works on the oil rigs and lives the life of a playboy when not working.

Johnny sees to his mothers needs the best way he can, they have a cleaner Pauline Trent a medium built dark haired young woman of 34 that comes in, in the mornings, her neighbour pops in now and again during the day, Mrs Laine, Jill Laine medium built fair haired 50 year old attractive lady, to see how Jean is keeping, they have been good friends for years! Mrs Laine has two sons, and a daughter, her daughter Susan a slim medium built 22 year old, a secretary at the local nick where Johnny is!! Jill's oldest son Shaun 17 yr old a slim medium built boy, interlect of the family is at college reading law, the youngest son Danny a big lad for a 15 yr old, with mousy hair a very good looking lad, a bit of a lad and a rouge! Jill's husband Jim a working man that works driving a bus for the local company Jim is a big strong dark haired man of 52 who just never has time off work! Danny goes round to see if Jean needs anything doing or from the shops, but Danny never does anything for nothing, a bit of a bully with younger kids or anybody he thinks he can bully, but quite opposite in front of his parents, you will nearly always find Danny well away from his home with his gang of followers, intimidating people he knows he can, like the young and old alike, they smoke wacky bacci and drink beer of any kind or anywhere, but mostly at a derelict building site, that's when they sometimes get little kids and beat them up for no reason at all, Danny will say to Jake who is a 14 year old autistic lad, " smack him and boot him Jake ", Jake will do that because he thinks Danny likes him and he'll be one of Danny's best mates.

Fury

To buy there drug needs and beer, they go and burgle and steal for money, one instance they were out late looking for somewhere they could brake in or a drunken bloke to rob, there were Danny, Jake, Pete, a medium fair hair lad 15 year old and Ricky on the small side with a rugged look a 14 year old! All four was sneaking up a path of a bungalow, they went through a gate to the backyard, smashed the kitchen window to get entry Jake and Ricky goes through the window, just as they entered into the kitchen, the kitchen door opened the light came on, an elderly gentleman that struggled to walk came in! When Ricky picked up the first thing he laid his hands on, a shovel he then hit the man on his head, whom went down on his knees bleeding, at that moment his wife came in who also struggled to walk, saw what had happened, she then collapsed to the floor in shock! By that time Danny and Pete had ran away, Jake and Ricky get back out through the window and take off after picking up a purse which was on the side of a work surface, as Danny and Pete was running away, a police patrol car, with two officers in, saw them and stopped, they asked Danny and Pete why they were running? At 11:30 in the evening, Danny said " home, were late in and we'll get into trouble "

"Where have you been?" asked one of the officers Pc Roger Dent a very tall man with dark hair, a rugged looking police officer "Out with our girlfriends", " that's not a crime is it?" the officer then said "Ok go on your way we don't want you to get into more trouble when you get home do we?"

The police and ambulance was called by Mrs Stobbard, the wife of the injured man, Mr Stobbard was taken to hospital with cuts and bruising and to be checked over incase of any other damage, one of the police officers Pc Harry George a dark haired well made copper, takes a statement from Mrs Stobbard, she gave a statement of events and a description what she could remember of the two intruders, but she explained she was very shocked and very nervous at seeing her husband Ted with a face and head full of blood.

At this time Jake and Ricky on there way down the road, was being passed by the police car and officers that had stopped Danny and Pete just a few minutes earlier! One of the officers Pc George Taylor said "Look Roger, two more little shitheads, should we stop them?" Roger replied "No we'll be going off duty soon!" "Yer your right , lets go and get off home".

Jake and Ricky soon found Danny and Pete at the derelict buildings where they hold up some of the time, Danny said, "What happened in the bungalow?" Jake told him, then Ricky said, "I managed to pick this purse up on the way out," Danny said "Give me it, lets have a look inside" there were £45 in notes and some change! Danny Said "I'll look after it now lets clear off I'll see you all tomorrow"

The following day at Mrs Longhursts home, with Pauline the cleaner doing her chores that Jean cant do anymore, and Johnny leaving for work "see ya later mum!"

"Bye John" Jean Answers, "be careful love"

John says "I will", Pauline finishing off her dusting "I'll make you a cup of tea before I go Jean, and fill you a flask if you need a drink later" when Jill Laine knocks on the door and enters "Hiya Jean how are you?" "Alright Jill! Johns just gone to work and Pauline's just making me a cup of tea before she goes"

"Just in-time then, no sugar for me Pauline!" Jill shouts, Pauline walks through into the room "Already made it I heard you come in Jill, I'm going now see you tomorrow Jean" "Thank-you!" Jean replies in a quite voice, Jean then looking at Jill "Anyway Jill it's nice to see you and its good of you to come and see me"

"No problem at all Jean"

"How are you Jill everything alright is it?"

"Well"… with a pause "I think so, except that our Danny was late in again, past midnight again!"

"Well you know what kids are like, they grow up so fast nowadays but I'm sure your Daniel is a good boy! You know Jill he's a bonny looking lad so he's bound to have a girlfriend or two!",

"Yes your probably right Jean", at this moment Danny knocks on the door and comes in "Hello Mrs Longhurst, just called in to see if you need anything from the shop or anything, oh hiya Mam"

"Yes Daniel could you bring me a loaf of thick sliced bread our John forgot it last night" Jean replied "Here's the money Daniel, what a good boy you have Jill it wont be long before he's a man will it Daniel?" Danny answers

"No Mrs Longhurst" then leaves "see you later"! His mother then shouts

"And don't be late in tonight"

"Ok Mam" After Danny leaves Jill says "You know Jean our Shaun is doing really well at college in his studies!"

"I think he will succeed Jill, he's a very intelligent young man answers Jean.

Meanwhile Danny goes to the shop for Mrs Longhurst, he meets Diane his girlfriend! A very pretty 14 year old with blonde hair he says "Diane if anybody like the cops comes to see ya' and asks if I was with you late last night say I was with you all night until about half past eleven!"

"Why" Diane asks

"Because me, Pete, Jake and Ricky have been out and about, and Jake and Ricky like idiots that they are, tried breaking into this place and nearly got caught! near where me and Pete was, they banged this old bloke on his head with a shovel!, nothing to do with me or Pete but you know what the cops are like they'll try and involve us because we was near the area, two coppers in a car stopped me and Pete to ask where we was going and where we had been because at the time we was running up the road I said I'd been with you, and Pete had been with Jacky, so you better tell her to do the same"

"Ok Danny will I, see ya' tonight"

"Yes" Danny answers "Look I've got to go now I'm doing an errand for Mrs Longhurst", and then Danny runs off up the road.

In the meanwhile at the local police station, the police dealing with the burglary of Mr and Mrs Stobbard's bungalow, Pc Adam Storey and Pc Paul Hartley, Pc Storey a 27 year old tallish man with brown hair, crew cut style smart looking copper and Pc Hartley a tall dark haired 27 yr old with a mushtash were talking to inspector John Hardy medium height darkish hair also with a mustash, a young looking 53 yr old! About the incident, when Pc Dent and Pc Taylor who had earlier stopped Danny and Pete, was walking by and heard a description that could had been Ricky North! They stopped and one of the officers Pc Dent said "We was in the area last night we stopped two lads as we was on our way back to the nick last night at about eleven thirty to ask where they had been and as we were on our way again we saw two other boys and one of the boys we passed sounded like that lad North's description, infact I'd seen him with the two lads we stopped before and one was Susan Laine's young brother Danny, I don't know the name of the other lad"

"Ok Roger" inspector says to Pc Dent "I'll see you later", inspector Hardy then to the officers Pc George and Pc Hartley, "Look I can tell you that the old gentleman Mr Stobbard is in a poorly condition and It could be more than just a burglary!, so you two go out there and make some urgent enquiries and get these kids in for questioning.

Danny just going back to Mrs Longhurst with a loaf of bread, going through the door, "There you are Mrs Longhurst got a thick sliced one for you, ill put it on the side in the kitchen"

"Thank you, here you are Daniel here's something for a few sweets or something" handing Danny a pound, then kissed him on his cheek,

"Thank you Mrs Longhurst"

"You're a good boy don't be late home for your mum!"

"Ok see you later Mrs Longhurst"

"See ya mam" Danny then trots off to see his mates,

"I don't know Jean" Jill says

"You shouldn't keep giving him a pound, that means your bread's cost you two pound!"

"That's alright Jill, you're only young once"

On his way Danny sees Jake, "Hiya Danny"

"Hiya" Danny Replies "Where you going?" Jake answers

"To see if I can find you Danny"

"Well you've found me, what the fuck do you want?"

"Will we be sharing that money out from last night?"

Fury

"If I had it, I would!" Danny says "I lost it on the way home, I probably dropped it out of my pocket when I was running so I wouldn't be too late in"

Jake says, "I needed some of that money, to buy a couple of bottles of cider!"

"Well you'll have to go nick some money from your granny wont ya? Or go and mug some old fart, plenty of old women walking around with there bags"

Looking at Jake, "Come on if your coming"

"Ok Danny" Jake like a lap dog following his master,

Back at the local nick chief super intendant Alan McClure a tall fair haired and small beard 47 yr old rugged looking chief, goes through into inspector Hardy's office to inform him news from the hospital, "John" says the chief!

"Yes sir",

"News…Bad news, Mr Stobbard has just died at the hospital after having a heart attack, now get these lads in john, that was seen in the area last night!"

"Yes sir, straight away", inspector Hardy goes with a brisk walk to the control room telling the girl on the switch board "Get a call out to Pc Dent and Pc Taylor to find this lad Ricky North and bring him in right away"

"Yes sir" she replied

Back to the corner where the gang meet up there is about nine or ten lads there all with baseball caps on some with hoods over their caps, when Danny and Jake arrive, Ricky says

"Have you got that money Danny?" Jake answers

"He's lost it on his way home last night" Ricky says

"Fucking hell, fucking great!" Danny then says

"What's that mean!" Ricky said

"Nothing except I could have done with a few quid"

"Ay Danny, did you hear about the big fire at Johnson's old food factory?" said one of the lads called Joe Downs a small 14-year-old fairish haired lad a little bully and a nasty person!

"No" answers Danny "What fire?"

"Ha it'll be in the paper tonight, we were there, there was about 30 of us, and some of the kids from the Barclay estate, somebody set fire to it, what a hell of a fucking fire, there were 3 fire engines but they couldn't do much straight away we all started throwing bricks and stones at them or anything we could find to throw, then the big boys from the blue brigade three cars and two meat wagons came flying down the road flashing there lights and blasting there fucking sirens thinking they thought we would all run off but we never we gave them some of the same we smashed a few windows on there cars and vans, but then we had to take off they caught two lads and slung them into a van"

"Sounds boring" Danny says, "What did you get for that?"

"What d'ya mean" Joe says "We got a fucking good laugh"

At that time the police car with Pc Dent and Pc Taylor coming down the road, "Hey" said one of the gang "Look who's pulling up here" they all looked when the police car came to a holt, the two police officers get out of the car, walked up to the lads, when Pc Dent said looking at Ricky North "North your wanted at the police station!"

"What for?" in a clever manner, the officer said

"Maybe something, maybe nothing, we just want to ask you some questions to eliminate you from our enquiries. We also want you as well" looking at Jake "Why? I ain't done nothing" Pc Dent Said

"Well in that case you've got nothing to worry about then have you, come on both of you in the car" Ricky gets in but Jake then says

" Ballocks I'm not going, Pc Dent says, come on George we'll take this one and have the other one picked up" Pc Dent looking at the gang and says "see ya lads, were bound to" the police then drove away.

Harry Pearce a 14 year old with brown long hair not a pretty sight a member of the gang said "Anybody know what that was all about?" Danny said

"Yes, Ricky and Jake did a burglary last night and it looks like they've been nicked!"

At Mrs Longhurst's Johnny comes in "Hiya mum"

"Hello love, how are you?"

"Ok mum, ill be working a little later tonight with the trouble with the fire at Johnson's old food factory. And there's been a burglary, where the old boy had an heart attack and died" what a carry on with these young slobs, we do this! That! And the other, when we pull them in what happens! They just seem to get away with it! Doing it again and get a slap on the wrist! They just seem to get away with nearly everything, they're just laughing at the system!

" Don't get too up tight John! There are still more good young people out there than bad!"

" I know that mum" Johnny replied, " Maybe I'm just tired ".

Back at the police station the two police officers arrive and take Ricky North into a interview room,

" Now then lad what have you and your friend been up to then?" Pc George Taylor asks Ricky North

" Nothing Ricky " remarks!

" Well me and my colleague Pc Dent saw you and that friend of yours near to Mr and Mrs Stobbard's bungalow! What was broken into! Where Mr Stobbard was hit over the head with a shovel! And has later died in hospital. And the shovel will be checked for prints and DNA! Now have you anything to say?

" Look I don't even know what you're talking about!" replies North

" Well look at it like this! It wont be just a robbery now, this could be murder your going to be in real shit now aren't you North?"

" Fuck you!" North shouts

" Well when we bring your mate in we'll know a bit more then won't we? In the meantime see you soon!"

Leaving Ricky in the room, when another police officer comes in and takes Ricky to the cells.

At the time Pc Dent and his partner pc Taylor was going to the house for Jake Ford. They knock at the door and Jakes father answers. John Ford a tall slim brown haired 39 year old on the social security!

" Yes? "what can I do for you! the officer Pc George says

" We would like to speak to Jake about a burglary last night "

John shouts! " Jake very loud, Jake come here now!" Jake comes to the door and Mr Ford says

" What's this about a burglary last night?" Jake answers by saying

" I don't know anything about a burglary last night!"

Pc George says " I think you do and you are as well helping us, and answering some questions with us down at the police station because it's more than just a burglary now it could be murder as well. Because Mr Stobbard the gentleman that was hit by a shovel has now died at the hospital"

" I didn't hit him "

" But you admit you where there with Ricky North who is now in custody " says Pc George,

" I kept telling you, you would get into trouble with the arse holes you hang around with didn't I? You flaming idiot " Mr Ford says in a FURY! At this time Pc George says " I'm arresting you at this time for suspected burglary " They then take Jake away. With some of the gang looking on! And shouting at the two police officers " police pigs ".

One of the gang Gerry Armstrong a fairish haired 14 year-old with a large birthmark on the side of his face! Says to the rest of the gang " I'm going to find Danny and tell him what's happened ".

Running up the street he bumps into Pete! Gerry shouts " come on we've got to find Danny " and Pete replies.

" What's up? "

" I'll tell you what's up on the way to Danny's "

Danny just walking through the door back home, Mrs Laine saying " oh Danny I'm pleased your home early your dad will be home from work soon! Put the kettle on for your mother please love "

" Ok mam " Danny replies, just as Jim, Danny's dad comes in the back door, he's a big, strong dark haired man of 52! " Hello son! "

" Hiya dad " Danny answers. Jill greets Jim with a kiss!

" What a day " he says " some idiot kids set fire to a factory, cops all over the place trying to find out the culprits! Every one you talk to says it was youths from the barclays estate! And some around this area have you heard anything about this Danny? "

" Yes dad but I don't know anybody from this area who had been there "

" Good " Jim replies " they must be sensible like you son! "

At the police station the two officers taking Jake in. Chief Super and inspector Hardy waiting! The chief says " ok have him in the charge room! "

Pc Dent taking Jake through. Pc Taylor explaining to him that Ford admitted to being at the bungalow but he did not do anything to Mr Stobbard

That was North " ok lets see him then we'll see north again " in the charge room chief Super, Alan McClure sits opposite Jake! " now then Jake depending if you are going to tell us precisely what happened depends what we will be charging you with! First and foremost the gentlemen mr Stobbard has died in the hospital! Now what are you going to tell us about this incident? You could be charged with just burglary or you could be charged with aggravated burglary, manslaughter or even murder. Now tell us the truth Jake! And we'll see what we can help you with ". Of course Jake spilled his guts he explains

" All I did was go through the window after Ricky when the light came on Ricky picked the shovel up and banged the old man over the head' with it "

" He says he was only half way in when that happened "

" And a old lady came in and we legged it! Ricky picked the purse up with some money inside before we got back out through the window! " Jake stated

" Where's the purse with the money in now? "

" Ricky gave it to Danny "

" Danny who? "

Jake said " Laine, Danny Laine "

" Was Danny Laine in the break in with you? " asks the chief

" No " said Jake " When we was running away we saw Danny and Pete "

" Pete who? " said the chief

" Pete Lawson " replied Jake

" And Ricky gave Danny it, right Jake we'll have another chat with you later. A police officer will bring you something to eat and drink if you want anything "

Jake then say's " Have you got a fag? "

" Sorry I don't smoke " then left the room. He then locates inspector Hardy and says " John you go and see North! See what he says and tell him we have already spoken to Jake "

" Yes sir will do "

Later at Danny Laines, Danny just leaving to go out " See ya' mam"

" Don't be late home Danny "

" I wont mam " and then leaves. Walking down the road to meet Diane he runs into Joe Downs! " Alright Danny where you off? "

" Why? " Danny asks!

" Just wondered that's all did you know that old bloke at the bungalow had died? "

" Hard fuck! It had fuck all to do with me! "

" The cops have been to Jakes and arrested him! An took him to the cop shop " says Joe

" So what? " Danny replies " and anyway I'm going to see Diane now and I ain't had it for a couple of days so I'll be busy, see ya' Joe "

" Yea ok Danny "

At the station inspector Hardy goes to see Ricky North inspector Hardy says, " now then north we've spoken to Jake Ford and he told us the full story of what happened at the Stobbard's bungalow! Now would you like to tell us in your own words what happened? " Ricky mouths off " what's that dick-head said to you? "

" Would you like to give us a statement? "

" I don't know what you're talking about! " answers Ricky!

" Ok north! We'll wait until we have the D-N-A from the shovel! And we will have them so why don't you make it easy on yourself and tell us the truth! " North looking a bit puzzled then said " O-k but I didn't mean to hurt that old man ok we broke in! The old man startled me when he came in through the door and turned the light on I just picked the shovel up to protect myself because he was coming towards me as though he was going to hit me I just protected myself "

Fury

" Ok North " said the inspector " I'll send someone in for you to make a statement, if you want a drink or anything just ask the officer ok? "

" Yeah " North replies. The inspector goes out and talks to pc Taylor and say's " George get your partner and I want you to pick up Danny Laine for questioning! You can get the address from the front desk! He happens to be Susan Laines brother ".

yes sir " replies Pc Taylor. Pc Taylor then went through to the canteen, saw Pc Dent and said " O Roger come on we've got to pick up Danny Laine and bring him in "

" Coming " Roger replies finishing his cup of tea as he is standing up. Walking through with his partner.

Danny walking with Diane up the street kissing and hugging, when Jerry and Pete shout " Danny wait we gotta tell ya' something, the cops have picked Jake up and took him to the police station " Pete say's

" Yeah I know I heard from Joe! " says Danny. " So what, what's it got to do with me? "

Pete says " yes I know know what Jakes like, he's an idiot and he'll say anything! "

" let him say what he wants! " Replies Danny " Let him try to implicate me, and he'll regret it! In more ways than one! "

" Where are you going now Danny? " Gerry asks,

" to get the leg over at Diane's! "

" Shut up Danny! Let everyone know! "

Danny laughing and saying " come on you silly cow "

At the station Susan Laine, sister of Danny. Walking through to see the inspector. Knocking on the door inspector Hardy says, " come in "

Susan walks in " yes Susan what can I do for you? "

" I just came to see you I heard you are looking for my brother Danny inspector Hardy "

" it's nothing to worry yourself over we just want to see if he can help us with an enquiry, apparently your Danny knows the two lads that we have brought in for burglary Ricky North and Jake Ford for what happened last night, only your Danny and one of his mates where stopped by two of my officers in the same area last night! We know your Danny has nothing to do with the burglary but he may be able to help us that's all Susan " inspector Hardy explained

" alright sir " and she then leaves.

on the road Pc Dent and Pc Taylor coming towards Danny and Diane, " George there's Danny Laine there with the girl "

" Yes " answers Roger " lets pick him up " they pull up near Danny and Diane Pc Dent gets out of the car and says " Danny Laine "

" Yes? What's the problem " asks Danny

" We just want you to come with me and my partner to the police station to clear one or two things up with our inquiry's about a burglary last night "

Danny says " I don't know what your talking about! what burglary are you on about I don't know about a burglary? I don't know about any burglary! "

Roger shouts! " We stopped you, me and my partner last night you was with your mate Pete Lawson! You were in the area of the burglary!"

" Yeah " said Danny, " well I told you me and Pete had Just left our girlfriends this is my girlfriend (Turning to Diane) where and who was I with all day yesterday Diane? "

Diane replied " Danny was with me all day and night until about 11:30 pm when he said he was late going home and then he left "

" there you are " Danny says " what else can I say unless you have a warrant accusing me of any part of your so-called burglary I'm not coming! I have nothing to be seen for ok come on Diane " but before Danny goes the officer said " what about a purse that North gave you last night? "

" What purse? " replies Danny " if anybody says they gave me a purse there lying! I know nothing about a burglary or a so-called purse " and started walking away with Diane then turned and said " any particular coloured purse? " and then turned round and started laughing along with Diane with his arm around her Danny Said " you did good there Diane lets go back to your place your mum and dads at

Fury

work so we can have an hour with each other doing what we like doing together " laughing.

Pc Taylor contacts the station to inform of the situation. " Control contacts! Inspector Hardy to speak to the two officers "
" Yes why could you not get him to come to the station, sir? "
Pc Taylor said he just would not come he has an alibi by his girlfriend and that he knows nothing about any burglary or about any purse "
" o-k George come back in "
" On our way sir over "
Back at the station chief super McClure goes through to see North to tell him that he and Jake will be taken to a secure unit for the time being with North just standing up and saying nothing the chief then goes through to see Jake and explains the same Jake starts crying and says " I want my mum "
The chief replies, " your parents will be informed "

Still at the station, Susan Laine bumps into Johnny Longhurst " hello Johnny "
" Hello Susan " Johnny replies
" Have you heard anything about my brother Danny!, apparently he is wanted to help the police with enquiries about some burglary and about two lads he knows who are now in the cells " Johnny replies by saying
" I don't know anything about it Susan I'm working on the fire that happened at the old food factory but I'll enquire for you and if I find anything out I'll let you know Susan "
" O-k thanks Johnny ".
At this time P.C Adam Storey was on his way to see Ricky North's and Jake Ford's parents and let them know about there sons being put into a secure unit, until they can put them in court! P.C Storey pulls up outside Ricky North's home where there is a gang of the usual yobs with Gerry Armstrong, Joe Downs, and Harry Pearse and about another nine or ten with them. PC Storey getting out of his car the yobs then start chanting abuse chanting little boy blue go blow your horn. You fucking nob-head. PC Storey says nothing just walks up

to the front door of the North's and knocks. Mr North comes to the door small fair-haired man " yes " he say's PC Storey says " Mr North " whom then replies

" What is the problem constable "

" Can I come in it's about your son Ricky! "

" Come in then " Mr North replied. PC Storey going into the house of the North's. With the gang still chanting! Gerry Armstrong says to Joe Downs " get that fucking brick and put it through the window of the Fucking coppers car! " straight away Joe picks up a house brick he runs across the road and throws it through the front window-screen of the police car at the same time the gang runs away cheering. Mrs North looked out of the window saw the shattered glass and the smashed window of the police car she says to the police officer " I think you better go out to see your car some-ones smashed the window-screen on it " PC Storey jumps up to go out to the car he see's what has happened and say's " I just don't believe it " repeating it over and over again I just don't believe it! he calls straight away to the station. The operating girl on the switchboard takes the call. The officer explains what had happened then the girl says, " Ok I'll report the incident control over ". Pc Storey in a slow voice " yeah over and out " standing there in disbelief! and shaking his head.

Later that evening, Johnny going through the front door " home, hello mum "

Jean replying " hello John you look a bit tired son! "

" I am mum " walking through to the kitchen " what would you like to eat mum? "

" Anything that's on the go love " Jean answers. " I'll make a cup of tea first " Jean says " there's still some hot water in my flask John! what Jill filled up for me earlier ok I'll use that and make a drink then, and I think I'll go to the fish and chip shop and I'll get us a fish an chip supper how's that mum? "

" That will be nice John "

" won't be long then " Johnny shouts

" Ok love " as Johnny is walking out of the door, on his way up the street on his way after walking about 25 yards, on the opposite side of the road he see's a gang of youth's with bats and pieces of wooden

Fury

railings, running and smashing car windows and screens. Johnny straight away on his mobile, phones the police to inform them of what was happening! They need to send some police down " there's too many of them for me to try and do anything about the situation there is about 15 – 20 just running and rampaging "

almost straight away a police car comes down the road with sirens and blue lights flashing. All the gang start scattering all over and running away, Johnny puts his arm up to stop the car. Two thickset policemen get out Johnny says " good job you lads came quick because god knows what they would have done next ", People coming out of their houses and to see what was happening and those who owned vehicles looking at the damage. Johnny says to the two police officers " look you will have to take over I have to go and get my invalid mother her supper " they said

" Ok sir we'll see to things " and Johnny says " ok I'll make a report tomorrow morning at the station " he then leaves. With the residents complaining about what's happening with these young thugs to the two police officers, one women say's " why should you even bother because when you catch them you just let them go again to do other damage to other people. Where is the law that used to be nowhere is it, look at my car " then starts crying with her husband putting his arm around her, other residents start complaining to the officers one man says " do you think we should get our own resident police force and see to these bastards because the law wont? "

Johnny back home to his mum going in the house Jean says, " was there a queue John you've been a while "

" No mum " he then explains what has happened Jean then replies

" Do you know John people cant feel safe anywhere anymore "

" Here you go mum eat your supper and we'll go to bed"

The following day at the youth court where Ricky and Jake are, the police tell the court that the two in court mentioned Ricky North and Jake Ford are being summoned for Jake aggravated burglary, criminal damage and manslaughter. And Ricky the same! On all the accounts, on the manslaughter charge be on the grounds that Mr Stobbard probably would not have died if he had not been struck down with the shovel that was used! Later the heart attack according to the court at this hearing decided that this case would have to go to the magistrates court with a date to be arranged until that time the police agree on bail. With both parties having to report to the police station daily at 4pm and both lads leave the court with their parents North looking very nasty towards Jake as they left.

At Mrs Longhurst's, neighbour Jill Laine having just made a cup of tea and sat down near Jean, when Jill say's " our Susan said the police wanted to see our Danny about some burglary what he knows nothing about except for being in the same area where the burglary took place! And the two they picked up for the crime it happens that our Danny knows them! " Jean says

" If all the kids was as good as your Daniel Jill they wouldn't be any problems at all! anywhere! "

" He's no angel Jean " Jill replies

" But he doesn't exactly get into trouble although he knows these thieves "

Jean says, " He's bound to know them though isn't he? He goes to school with these kids ".

At Jakes home with his mother and father Mr Ford talking to Jake

" Look boy when you go to court I want you to tell them the truth to the court if you had broken into the bungalow that was the only crime you did! Tell all o-k lad "

" O-k then dad " Jake answered. Jakes uncle then came in

" Hey Billy! " Mr Ford shouted

" hay-up John what's the problem then? I could hear you from outside! ".

John then explained the situation to his brother Billy! A tall and slim 43 year-old man with a rugged looking face. " look Jake the sooner you stop hanging around with scum like who you knock around with! The better it'll be for yourself, just get it into your head Jake otherwise you'll finish in the gutter and with nothing! Like they'll finish up with. Years ago when we were younger me and your dad, we wouldn't even think about it what these pricks do now you think Jake that they will only do things in a gang on their own they are like yellow bastards. So for your own good Jake keep away from them please! " Billy explained the situation clearly

" Ok uncle Billy I will ".

The following day kids leaving school and walking down the road towards the derelict buildings, There's Danny and all the gang meeting up Danny says to Jake " involve me in this Fucking episode with the law! I can tell you I'll fucking knock you dafter then you already are do you understand

Jakie boy? "

" Yeah sure Danny I wouldn't say anything about you at all! " Jake replied nervously. Joe Downs then runs in towards the gang " Hey lads " he says

" Look here at that silly old cunt who's wheeling that shopping trolley she can hardly walk but look where she's got her handbag! On her arm lets go get

It! " Danny says

" Go on Joe get it for us you can manage it on your own go with him Harry one distract her and one grab it! " so they did. They took off after the women Joe and Harry running towards her! Joe runs up to the lady gives her a smack right in the face grabs her bag and yanks it from her arm and pulling her down then Harry boots her in the face they then take off back to where the rest are when they enter Danny says " What ya' got? "

Joe says, " I don't know but it feels heavy " Danny says

" Give me it now " lets have a look " there's a purse with about £200 with change, a pension book and other papers, Danny says " where's the house keys we could have gone and wrecked the fucking place " Joe says

" Keep looking in the bag see if there in there " Danny then say's to him by saying " don't worry we know where she lives anyway her address is in the pension book, we'll just keep a look out for her " Joe says

" O-k then Danny let me have some money " Danny replies

" Here then, you can have £50 for you Harry and £50 for you Joe I'll take £50, then throws the rest down and said " and you lot can share that " Danny then looks and says to Pete " I'm off Pete I'll see you on Saturday, I'm going home for tea and then I'm off to see Diane tonight where babysitting her little brother " then he runs off laughing. All the other kids dive in for what they could get Jake leaves looking on and looking worried and the rest are just laughing Joe says " come on lets go and spend some of this money ".

Later at the police station inspector Hardy goes through to the desk, walks up to the desk sergeant Paul Stretton " Paul! " inspector Hardy shouts " I need to see you a minute, There's been trouble an old lady Gladys Stones has been beaten up and robbed while walking down Lime Road going to the shops at about 4:20pm somebody has been to see her in hospital but she cant give any description she said it all happened to fast she was hit and kicked in the face and so far there is no witnesses, the ambulance had been and taken her straight to hospital she is badly bruised, blood shocked eyes and a busted top lip this at this moment we don't know if there is any other injury's! what's happening Paul in this country of ours it'll have been youths, young kids, druggies or both that I believe be the culprits, what do you think to an 80 year-old person what will parents think of these thugs of theirs what will they probably say? ". Inspector Hardy looking very annoyed " our Jimmy or Tommy wouldn't do a thing like that! " Sergeant Stretton a tall copper of 34years a slim built person says " sir if you don't mind me saying off the record we just haven't got the man power to see to things quick! break in's burglary most of the time the people that phone in to inform us they have been burgled what do we do? We give them a crime number and hope they are insured "

" Paul " Inspector hardy shouts " what about the trauma for these innocent people with closing a lot of police stations, some just open during the day! And one main station open all the time, sometimes when people need us they could be in a village 20 or 30 miles away or even more! where they have a local bobby how long would it take to get them there! There have been complaints upon complaints that when people phone up for assistance by the police they are often waiting in

Fury

a queue with music what's that supposed to do sooth them! but what can we do about it? "

" We do what we can do " Paul answers " any way sergeant I just wanted to get things off my chest well some of it anyway Paul I think I'll have a cup of tea "

" You do sir "

Inspector Hardy walking away " Yes sir I do know what your saying Paul in a quiet voice ".

A few days go by, Ricky North and Jake Ford have already been to the magistrates court. Jake was found guilty of attempted burglary and got a fine of £120. Ricky was found guilty of burglary and criminal damage and he also got fined £250 but he was found not guilty as he acted in self defence and not guilty of manslaughter it was apparently the old gentlemen Mr Stobbard had a series of heart problems having already having two heart attacks in the period of nine months said the barrister! North had pleaded guilty to burglary and criminal damage but not guilty to manslaughter on the grounds of self defence although North and Jake where deeply sorry that Mr Stobbard had, had an heart attack but North's barrister said " Ricky could not be blamed and be made responsible "so they did well by more or less of getting away with what happened.

Back at Mrs Longhurst's house with Johnny making a cup of tea for his mum and himself. Johnny comes through into the room with the tea and sits down with Jean and she says, " How are you John? You look miles away! "

" Oh do I mum I didn't realise I probably am the two lads who broke into that bungalow where that old man had an heart attack and died in hospital was at court today and got away with just a fine, things like this peeves me off badly, "I feel sorry for his wife! She's got to live with what happened she's in her seventies and if she stays where she is, she's on her own now! I'm sure she will have someone to take care of her John " answers Jean.

" Maybe so mum but it effects the whole family of what and how things occurred something they will never forget no matter what happens in the future this will always be on their minds ".

Then a knock on the door comes, the door opens and in comes Danny " hello Mrs Longhurst would you like anything doing at all? Oh hello Johnny " Danny says " Hello Danny " Johnny replies

" No I wont need anything tonight thank you Daniel Johns brought home everything we need "

" Ok then Mrs Longhurst " but before Danny leaves as he is opening the door " Danny " Johnny shouts " did or have you heard anything about an old lady being beaten up and mugged? "

" No Johnny I haven't " Johnny then to the reply from Danny,

" Oh that's alright Danny I just thought if you had heard anything, if you do find anything or hear anything I would appreciate it "

" Yes o-k Johnny " Danny then leaves and says as he walks outside the door " bye both of you "

" See you, bye Daniel " Jean replies. Danny then leaves walking along meeting Diane " hi Di " Danny said, grabbing her putting his arm round and kissing her she smiles at Danny and says " I love you Danny "

" Yea I know you do because I love you too! " Danny replies walking hand in hand as they run into Pete and Jackie Webb, Pete's girlfriend a smallish red head of 14 " did you hear about what happened at court today with Ricky and that dope Jake spilling his guts and blaming Ricky for everything! " Pete says to Danny

" Yea I know I heard his old man told him what to say he blamed Ricky for everything and the idiot got away lightly, good job he never said anything about us eh? "

" Yea but he still needs sorting out though! "

" Ricky will sort him out " says Danny! they go to the derelict buildings then where they all seem to meet up, just walking in some rubble there's about 30 kids there. About half from the Barclay's estate when one lad from the Barclay area stood out a big lad called Jason Anderson a tall 15 year-old brownish hair and a rugged looking lad and he says " Alright Danny? " and Danny says

" What the fuck are you lot doing here? "

Fury

" Well you know we've just come around to help you lot run a riot in your area and how to put the fucking shits up people! " Danny then says

" We don't need you lot trying to take over round here so you can all fuck

Off! " Jason then says

" Look Danny boy I haven't come out here to fall out with yea, if you say you want us to fuck off then we will. Only some of your mates was with us when we set fire to the old food factory when we all gave some of the coppers and fireman some brick bruising ". Jason then turns to his gang and shout, " OK COME ON LADS, see yea Danny "

" Yea ok Jason " after the Barclay's lot go Joe Downs says.

" You put him fucking right Danny the fucking wanker "

" Look Joe if I were you I wouldn't let Jason hear you call him a Wanker " Danny looking across at Ricky North, " You alright Ricky? "

" Yea I'm alright Danny I will be if I get my hands on Jake the fucking rake "

" Yea " Joe shouts " lets get the fucking bastard " Danny says " Joe you know that Jakes got a rabbit right "

" Yea " Joe replies

" Well why don't you and Ricky go and nick it out of its cage "

" Yea Ricky lets go get it then we can chop its fucking head off come on Ricky " as he taps him on his shoulder " We wont be long " Ricky says and leaves with Joe.

Back at the Laines house Jill just getting her husband Jim's supper ready as Jim walks in " Phew what a day "

" What's the matter Jim " Jill asks

" What's the matter what a day it's been the driver on 64 route, has he's leaving the last stop on the Barclay's estate a gang of kids start throwing bricks and stones through the windows he's a nervous wreck and so is some of the passengers he radioed for some help but heading straight away for the depot he saw nobody for help " Jim says disgustedly. Then Jill says

" Where was the police at this moment? "

" I don't know you tell me what a carry on! this place isn't safe anymore "

Jill then says, " I'm pleased you're not on that run Jim I'd be worried everyday "

" Yea but what about the poor sods that is, but if things keep happening like this on that route the drivers will refuse to do it ". Jim sitting down at the table to eat his supper " has our Danny been in yet? " Jim asks

" No " Jill answers " he's out with Diane "

" Good I'm pleased our Danny's not like them pieces of shit, down where Jake lives! down the passage to the back of his house.

Joe and Ricky go up the path to near the back door where the rabbit hutch is. They take the rabbit out of its cage and then take off towards the derelict buildings but the only people that where there was Pete Lawson and his girlfriend Jackie, Danny and Diane and a couple more kids drinking cider!

" Here Danny we got it " Joe says holding the rabbit by it's ears

" What are you going to do with it now then? " Danny questions Joe and Ricky. Joe then picks up a house brick, holds the rabbit by its body and slams the brick on the rabbits head and says that's what, Danny's girlfriend Diane says " You rotten bastard Joe what did you have to go and do that for? " Diane screams " Well we'll let Jake have it back now " and walks away laughing.

The following day Jake goes out of the door and see's his pet rabbit gone he runs back in and tells his dad his rabbit had gone Jakes dad says " someone's probably let it out! But it may have gotten out itself if the cage was not shut properly, I'll have a look around and ask the neighbours if they have seen anything now your going to have to go to school now Jake so go on, I'll have a look I promise just keep away from the shit-heads "

" OK dad ". Then Jake leaves for school, Mr Ford then goes looking around and asking neighbours if they have seen their pet rabbit, whoever

Fury

he asks nobody has seen anything but still continues looking. Lillian Ford the wife of John and the mother of Jake is on her way home from her early morning cleaning job Lillian is a smallish dark haired 38 year old lady says " What's the matter John looking for the rabbit either some ones let it out or took it out of the cage or it just could be that the door wasn't shut properly, has our Jake gone to school? "

" Yes " replies John

" Come on then John lets have a cup of tea "

" No I don't want one yet Lillian I'm going to keep looking ".

Later at school at dinner time just outside of the school gates Jake stood talking to some kids when Danny had walked up to him and said " Hi Jake "

" Alright Danny " Jake replied

" Has anything been happening Jake? "

" No not really except me rabbits gone "

" Your rabbit, I saw Joe Downs and Ricky with one last night but I don't think it'll be yours Jake "

Jake says " why it could be and he's took it from my cage I don't know "

Danny says, " why don't you ask him when you see him "

" Yea you know, I will " Said Jake. Jake on his way home at teatime leaving school he see's Joe, Danny, Ricky and a few more, Joe says " Lost ya rabbit Jake ".

" Yea Danny said you had a rabbit is it mine? "

Joe says, "It might be" laughing, " I'll bring it round later "

" Yea ok Joe thanks mate " Jake replies. Jake gets home and then tells his dad " Joe might have the rabbit he said he's going to bring it round later "

Mr Ford says, Well if it is what is he doing with it? " Jake answers

" I don't know dad " Lillian Ford Jakes mother shouts

" John there's a gang of kids outside shouting Jake ". John and Jake come running through to the front door John opens the door and Joe Downs shouts " Here Jake I've got your rabbit well at least its head " Joe had chopped the animals head off! And he throws it at the window when John goes outside and screams," what do you think your doing you set of scum " walking towards them! Joe he takes a baseball bat from one of his gang friends and runs towards Mr Ford he then whacks it on John's shoulder just missing his head then whacks him again on his back. Jake then comes running towards what was happening when four other kids get him and punched him to the ground kicking both him and his father Lillian comes running out " I've phoned the police now leave them alone "

" Look! you can fuck off Mrs or you can have the same, " says one of the gang members. Looking from a distance Danny goes! laughing to himself. Mrs Ford goes back into the house and phones for an ambulance and then calls Billy, Johns brother to tell him what had happened she then goes back outside! the gang of kids start running away some neighbours come out to help Mr Ford, helping both John and Jake up from the ground as the ambulance is coming down the road the ambulance comes to a halt the medics help John and Jake into the ambulance John with a badly cut face with pains in his back and shoulder and Jake has a bruised and cut face the ambulance leaves as the police car is coming down the road! And they pull up outside the Fords, With Lillian stood outside with some neighbours. The two police officers get out the car, PC Adam Storey and PC Paul Hartley to see Mrs Ford to find out what had happened and to get a full statement from Mrs Ford.

Back at Danny's home, Danny just going in the back door " hiya mum "

" Hiya Danny " his mother answers " I'm pleased your home early it's nearly six o'clock and ya" dad will be home soon "

" Right mum I'll just go to Mrs Longhurst to see if she wants anything doing "

" all right Danny but don't be long "

" O-k mum " and Danny leaves walking along the road on his way to Mrs Longhurst's, on his travels he see's Ricky " hiya Rick! "

" hiya Danny " Ricky replies " ya' hear about what's happened at Jakes " Ricky asks

" Yea I've heard " replies Danny

" they had to take Jake and his dad to hospital ya' know Danny Joe's a bit of an idiot for doing what he did " as Danny replies

" Yes but it was Jake and his dad that gave you a bad word "

" yea maybe your right Danny but sometimes it could go too far "

" Or leave it Ricky! look I've got to go I'm just nipping to see if Mrs Longhurst needs anything "

" O-k Danny "

" yea see you Ricky "

Danny arriving at Mrs Longhurst's knocking on the door and then going inside.

"Hello Mrs Longhurst do you need anything doing?"

"I wouldn't mind if you could just put the kettle on for me and make a cup of tea for me Daniel until our John comes home from work please Daniel"

"Ok" says Danny after putting the kettle on walking back into the room"

"Anything else Mrs Longhurst?"

"No Daniel thank you" looking at Mrs Longhurst and says

"Why don't you get someone to take you out more in the wheelchair and get some colour back into your cheeks Mrs Longhurst, with warmer weather now!

"That's nice of you to think about me Daniel" says Jean

"Yea maybe I should if you like I could maybe take you out for a walk for an hour or so now and again"

"Well thank you Daniel you're a lovely, honest boy maybe that will be nice you're a very caring boy you are Daniel I must tell our John of your offer and of course Jill your lovely mother"

"Your kettles boiled now Mrs Longhurst I'll just make you a cup of tea" when Danny comes back through with the drink he puts it down on the table so Mrs Longhurst could reach out and get it

"Alright Mrs Longhurst I'm going now if there wont be anything else you want me too do"

"O-k Daniel come here and have this pound to get something with" passing it to Danny

"Come here pet" and kisses Danny on the cheek, then Danny kisses Jean on her cheek

"Oh Daniel that was nice of you" he then leaves.

Soon afterwards Johnny comes in the door, Jean tells of Danny's offer, John replies by saying "That's good of him mum, as long as he's careful"

Jean then says " he's a fairly big and a strong boy I'm sure I'd feel safe with him"

At the police station both Pc Storey and Hartley, reporting to inspector Hardy says

"Look as soon as we have a written and signed statement from Mr Ford then we'll see these yobs!"

"Yes sir" they then leave.

Later, very late in the evening a gang of about 25 lads and girls down Seton road, a back road near the local pub at about eleven thirty pm, most of the gang was from the Barclay estate and amongst them was Joe Downs, Harry Pearse and Gerry Armstrong and a few of Joe Downs scummy mates! Along with Jason Anderson the leader of the Barclay lot. Just standing around throwing stones, at certain peoples windows mostly the elderly people who is too frightened to go outside. Jason says to Joe

"Hear you battered a bloke and one of your own mates Joe, he then replies by saying

"He's one of our mates but he's just a shit head mouthing to the police like his old man told him too but its got them nowhere, trying to blame our mate Ricky North for everything" at that moment one of the gang said

"Hey, look who's staggering down the road, that clever bastard from that second hand shop, one of the girls says

"Lets smack him one" another one of the gang said

"Yea lets get him" so they all started running towards him shouting anything from get the bastard to come here you fucking cunt where coming to batter you! You miserable old fart, as they approached him one of the gang hit him in the face another dived on his back pulling him down on the road they all started kicking him and one of the girls stamped on his head then Joe says

"Give me some of the action" when booting him in the face then jumped on his head. The man looked to be in very bad shape, the gang then started running up the road chanting die you fucking arse hole.

Some neighbours came out of there houses onto the road, 2 men went to the man to see if they could help and one of the men shouted
"Somebody phone for an ambulance and the police" the man laying on the ground looked critically damaged with blood running out of his mouth and his ears, an old lady comes out and brings a blanket for the man, the two men with him talking to him trying to make him stay awake which was very hard to do with him being in such a state, his eyes open looking not really knowing what has happened, after a few minutes pass an ambulance with the blue light and siren going comes rushing down the road and stops where the man is laying, the two medics rush to him to have a look at what they are dealing with, one of the medics says to his partner
"Get the stretcher" the medic with the man on the ground turned to the people that was looking on
"What the hell has happened here?" as a police car is coming, blue lights and a siren going one of the men said
"There was a gang of about 30 kids that did it, they beat him up bad" the medics get the injured man on the stretcher and getting him into the ambulance the two police officers Pc Dick Charmer a medium build 25 year old with brownish hair a good looking medium height copper and Stan Smith a very rugged looking 29 year old Blonde hair and tallish looked at the man getting in on the stretcher
"Who the hell could do this to an old man" asked PC Charmer! soon afterwoods the ambulance with lights and siren going take off to the hospital.
Police officer Stan Smith said to the 2 men who had tried to help the old man
"What's been happening here then" the one of the two men said
"About 30 kids beat him" the officer then said
"Does anybody know why?" the men answered
"No" Pc Charmer said
"Did anybody recognise any of the culprits" the answer was no they said

"We didn't know what had happened until we came out and saw the man laying on the road and a gang of kids running away chanting obscene words" Pc Smith Said

"Ok can we take your names and address" to the two men

"Just incase we need to come and see you" they gave the police their details.

A day later the police had already been to see Mr Ford at the hospital and had a statement naming Joe Downs the culprit and ring leader of the incident, leading to both Mr Ford and Jake needing treatment. Pc Storey and Pc Hartley talking to Inspector Hardy

"Right then Adam you better get off with Paul and bring this thing in for questioning"

"Yes sir" and away they went.

Still at the station Johnny going through to the office and says

"Sir, I've been making some enquiries about the smashing of car windows down near me in Oriel Street as I said I didn't recognise any of them there was talk around that it was some kids from the other side of town, I suppose we'll never find these kids out"

"Probably not Johnny but now I want you to look into last nights beating of an old chap a Mr Steve Hanley by a large group of kids on Stanley Road late last night there is a couple of addresses of two men who came out to Mr Hanley while he was laying on the road also for you to go see the man at the hospital"

"Alright sir"

"And Johnny" the Inspector says

"Let me know of anything you can find out as soon as possible no matter how small"

"Yes sir will do"

"See you later Johnny".

Later that day at Mrs Longhurst's where Jean is sat talking to Jill Laine when a knock on the door and Danny comes in

"Hello Mrs Longhurst" very polite like Danny is

"Hiya mum"

"Hello Daniel" Mrs Longhurst answers

"Hiya Danny" from his mum

"Do you need anything doing Mrs Longhurst"
"Not today Daniel but thank you for coming"
"If you like Mrs Longhurst with it being Saturday tomorrow if you want I could take you to the shops in your wheelchair"
"That would be very nice Daniel and thank you again"
"What time would you want me to come?" Danny Asks
"Well if you could possibly make it for about nine thirty Daniel our John will be going to work for about that time" Danny replies
"That'll be ok Mrs Longhurst" walking to the door
"See you then, see ya mum" and Danny leaves. After Danny had left Jean says to Jill
"Isn't he a thoughtful lad! sometimes Jean"
"I just wish he would come home earlier at night" Answers Jill

Danny walking along down the road, he bumps into Pete and Jackie
"Hiya Pete"
"Hiya Danny" Pete replies
"How ya doing Jackie"
"Alright Danny" Jackie replies
"Is he looking after you, if he ever don't come and see me" when Diane walks up she says
"Come and see you Danny what for?"
"Don't be silly Diane just a bit of fun"
"It didn't sound like it"
"Your too suspicious Diane!" Pete then says
"Did you hear about last night an old bloke got really beat up by about 20 kids mostly from the Barclay estate but guess who was there with them?"
Danny says
"Probably Joe"
"Yes, what a plonker" Pete says, then coming down the road Joe Downs and Harry Pearse both doing wheelies at the wrong side of the road heading towards traffic, a car and a van coming up the road. The driver of the car can't believe what he sees he starts slowing down the bikes still coming towards him. The van behind must think the car in front is slowing down to stop and with no traffic coming the other way

the van pulls out to overtake the car. Joe pulls out into the middle of the road and the van having to swerve and miss him Joe turns on his bike and shouts at the van driver

"Silly bastard you nearly hit me!" the car has come to a halt by this time, Harry shouts at the driver

"What you looking at you silly bastard" Harry shouts!

"What the fuck are you silly cunts trying to do! Said Danny when walking towards Joe and Harry, down the road is Billy Ford the brother of course to John and uncle to Jake walks up to Joe Downs and says

"You! You little bastard you haven't got a gang with you now why don't you try the same on me as you did with my brother" Joe runs towards him takes a swing at Billy but misses, at that time Billy hits Joe head on in his face Joe staggers then Billy hits him again, Joe go's down to the ground bleeding, Danny says

"Leave him alone do you know your in trouble now hitting an under age 13 year old kid!" Billy says

"See! Rules for such shit as him and a lot more like him because they are under age, that's ok is it!? They can go round beating people up because they are braver in there gangs! Not so much on there own are they! The set of yellow bastards!!" at this moment a police patrol car coming down the road, Danny puts his hand up to stop the patrol car in which stopped. The two officers Pc Dent and Pc Taylor get out of the car and said

"Whats happened here then" Danny says

"This bloke just came up and smacked Joe in the face, Joe is only thirteen how old will this bloke be!" Pc George Taylor said

"Is that right sir?"

"Not quite" says Billy

"It was this little bastard and his mates that beat my brother and nephew up, my brother still in hospital and this little shit took a swing at me so I acted in self defence" Pc Dent says to Joe

"How are you?" Joe says

"I'm alright I haven't done anything he's lying he just came up and hit me"

"That's right officer" Danny replies, Pc Dent says

"Right sir you will have to come to the station with us and you lot will have to come up to make a statement! alright, my colleague will

Fury

take your names and addresses and we'll expect to see you sooner than later, alright boys and girls" the police then leave with Billy Ford to the station, Danny says to Joe

"You better get things right what your going to say before we go to the cop shop wont you"

"Come on Diane lets go, we'll walk down with you Danny" says Pete

"Ok come on"

Joe and Harry head off on there bikes meeting up with some of the usual gang of clown's on the corner of Danby Road a main road area, Joe sees Gerry Armstrong

"Hiya Gerry" Joe shouts riding towards him

"Now then Joe who's been using your face as a door"

"That bastard Jake's uncle Billy Ford the cops have taken him to the slop shop to see why he hit me with no just cause" when Joe said that the gang started laughing Gerry said

"At least the law is on your side your under age" at this time Danny and Diane along with Pete and Jackie was just walking up to them when Gerry said,

"look what's walking up the street, a mongee!" the lad was a teenage down syndrome Joe chants

"Hay mongee come here what ya got to give us so I don't smack you in the face" at this time two young lads from the sixth form at the same school as most of the gang that is there stood like vampires Jimmy Hackett and Shaun McClure, Jimmy a tallish fifteen year old with brownish hair and a rugged looking lad with Shaun another tallish fifteen year old, a smart looking lad Jimmy said looking at Danny

"You don't knock around with these nob heads do you Danny" Danny answers

"They don't do anything bad they just like a bit of fun"

"Is that what you think Danny" Jimmy said then walking away the two lads said to the downs syndrome teenager

"Come on mate walk up with us you'll be alright" Shaun said

"What's ya name mate?" the teenager about seventeen year old said

"My names Gary" the teenager who is friendly with anybody and everybody like these lads are! Gary said"

"Thank-you I was very frightened I don't know how to fight if they had hit me" Jimmy says

"Ah come on" walking well around from the corner

"No one will touch you their idiots they only fight or should I say bully when they're in a gang don't you worry go home now" They part company and say goodbye.

At the police station Billy ford making a statement to Pc Taylor Billy admitting hitting Joe Downs but also stating it was pure self defence

"The lad took a swing at me, I dodged he missed and I hit him he came again at me so I hit him again what was I supposed to do let him do what the hell he liked these shit heads like him think because they are under 16 they can do and get away with things but the way the law is they can!" Pc Taylor said

"At the moment its going to be difficult for you Mr Ford, them lads are going to have the same story and say you just came up and hit him without anybody seeing what happened in your favour I cant say anymore until we see all statements from the boys right Mr Ford you'll be hearing from us until then you are free to leave I would advise you keep away from them alright Mr Ford"

"O-k constable what you say is if I see them in the distance go another way to avoid them in that case ill be hiding so they can carry on as normal being the scumbags they are!" Billy then leaves.

Billy on his way home down the road where the incident happened there's an old boy stood near the front gate of his home, his name is Jack Dowse a smallish man of eighty one years old a very quite thinning grey haired man he says

"Hello Billy I saw what happened and that Joe Downs got his just deserve"

"Look Jack" Billy said to Mr Dowse

"Can you give a statement at the police station to state you saw precisely what happened because all them little bastards are going to have the same story"

Fury

"To blame me, I don't know Billy if they find out about me I'm going to suffer along with my wife who has alzimers I don't think I could cope" at this point one of the gang members was passing and heard what was being said

"But alright Billy I'll make a statement for you"

"Thank-you Jack I'll see the police and ask if they can come and see you"

"Alright Billy but I'll be frightened about it and what will happen by these kids they've no respect for anything" then Billy left saying

"Don't worry these things will be alright Jack"

Terry Smith the lad who heard Billy and Mr Dowse talking saw Joe Downs, Gerry Armstrong, Danny and Jason Anderson from the Barclay estate

"Hay! Joe heard something you'll be interested in" Terry told them everything he heard, Joe said

"Right that old bastards windows going in!" Danny said

"Well I wont be going to the cop shop to make any statement I think none of us should now and if I was you Joe I wouldn't go and smash any windows in yet, but that's up to you Joe"

The next day at the police station Johnny Longhurst comes through to go to inspector Hardy's office, knocking on the door and Johnny walks in seeing the inspector

"Morning Sir"

"Hello Johnny come right in, well Johnny"

"Right Sir, I've seen the guy a Mr Hanley" Johnny looking at his notebook

"He couldn't identify any of the gang that beat him up" Johnny says

"Its possible he had too much to drink"

"Maybe so, look Johnny I want you to go and see John Ford and Jake Ford to get a full statement of what really happened, though take detective constable Ivor Jones, Walking through the canteen Johnny sees Ivor

"Ivor" says Johnny, Ivor turns

"Hiya Johnny"

Don Fleming

"Ivor you come with me inspector Hardy wants us to get a complete statement from Jake and his father! on what happened to them"

"Right Johnny".

Later at the Fords, Ivor knocks on the door Johnny looking at about six yobs across the street, Mrs Ford opens the door, Ivor says

"This is detective sergeant Longhurst and I am detective Jones, can we see Mr ford and Jake Ford please" Mrs Ford answers

"Come in wont you" they both enter the house and close the door after themselves.

One of the gang Harry Pearse left the rest to find Danny to tell him what is happening, running up the road he sees Joe and Gerry he stops and says to Joe

"You better get some of the lads and lasses to say you were somewhere else when old man and Jake Ford got a belting because the cops are at there house now, I'm going to find Danny he might be able to come up with something ok"

"Right o" Joe replies.

Back at the Fords, Mrs Ford comes through from the kitchen

"I've brought a pot of tea if you would like one" to the two detectives, they both answer

"Thank-you Mrs Ford" Mr Ford tells the police what happened and what they did to Jakes pet rabbit

"It was mostly Joe Downs he cut off and through the rabbits head at us as I and Jake went out to the gate Joe Downs came at us and hit me on the shoulder with a baseball bat then the rest of them joined in with the beating, that Joe Downs wants sorting real good, more than likely sir but we have to do things by the law Johnny answers, what law, says Mr Ford.

The following day almost nine thirty Danny just going to Mrs Longhurst's knocking on the door and walks in

"Hello Mrs Longhurst"

"Hello Daniel, you are punctual Daniel, if you could just help me put my scarf on, our John put my coat on for me before he left for work, after Danny putting Jean's scarf on,

"Right Mrs Longhurst ready, and off we go"

"Get the keys and lock the door Daniel" Danny does that and off they go heading towards the shops when Gerry walks up

"Hiya Danny, Hello Mrs Longhurst" Jean says

"Hello young man" Gerry says

"I'll see you later Danny some news to tell you"

"Ok" Danny says to Gerry and off Danny goes pushing Jean in the wheelchair.

At the nick Chief Super Alan McClure sends word out to see Johnny Longhurst and Ivor Jones, Johnny enters after knocking on the chiefs door

"You sent for us Sir"

"Yes Johnny you and Ivor to go and pick up Joe Downs for him to come and make a statement about this Ford incident, I've read the statement of Mr Ford now we need to see Joe Downs"

"Yes Sir we'll leave straight away"

"Ok Johnny"

"I want to know as soon as you come back"

"Yes Sir"

On the street Gerry nearing the corner where most of the yobs are, sees Pete Lawson with his girl friend Jackie and Diane, Danny's girlfriend Gerry says

"Have you seen Joe" all say no they haven't seen him when Harry Pearse walking up Gerry says

"Have you seen Joe" Harry says

"Yes just left him we've made an alibi for him he was with Joyce Allison at the time when he belted old man Ford and Jake and I saw them together"

"Ok I'll go with that I was with you at the time"

Johnny and Ivor pulling up outside Joe Down's house getting out and going towards Down's front door. Knocking on the door Joe Downs answers the door, he says

"Yea?" Johnny identified himself and Ivor, and says
"Joe Downs?" Joe answers
"Yea!"
"We would like you to come to the station in connection with the assault on Mr John Ford and Jake Ford"
"What connection I don't know anything about it except what I've heard with talk what's going round" at this time Mrs Downs comes to the door
"What's the matter?" Joe says
"These two policeman want me to go to the police station about that beating of Mr Ford And our mate Jake they think I know something about it and I don't"
"If Joe says he doesn't know anything about it he wont, he's not a liar" Johnny then says
"We have a statement from Mr Ford and he's implicating Joe as the main suspect so the thing is Mrs Downs we have been sent to pick Joe up and take him to the station to make a full statement to say if he was not their, whom he was with and who saw him, if anyone, you may come with him or any one person may accompany Joe all we need is a statement then he can come back home"
"That sounds alright Joe I'll come with you let me get my coat on"

At this time Danny just coming back with Mrs Longhurst, unlocks the door opens it and pushes Mrs Longhurst in the house.
"Daniel can you just put me the shopping in the kitchen our John will put it away" Danny does that then Jean says
"Can you just help me off with my coat Daniel" in which he does
"If you could just get me a cup and some milk Daniel I have hot water in my flask so I can have a cup of tea"
"I'll do that for you Mrs Longhurst" in which he does quite well
"Right Mrs Longhurst I'll go now and get my tea"
"Thank-you Daniel and here's a fiver you deserve it"
"No it doesn't matter"
"Take it Daniel I want you to" so Danny takes it" Jean kisses Danny on the cheek like she usually does and says
"I'll see you probably tomorrow or whenever Daniel alright"

"Alright Mrs Longhurst" and kisses Jean on the cheek also
"Bye" Danny says
"Goodbye Daniel"

Danny leaving to go home for his tea and sees Pete with Jackie
"Hiya Pete, Hiya Jackie"
"Hiya Danny" they both answer, Pete says
"Have you heard Joe got picked up by the law and taken to the cop shop with his mother"
"No!, do they suspect his mother as well" Laughing as he his saying it
"No but we have an alibi for Joe"
"Well I hope you haven't entered me to part of his alibi"
"No but I thought I would tell you"
"Ok Pete" Danny answers
"Also Danny! Diane says! will you be seeing her tonight" Jackie asks
"I don't know I'll see her if I go out, anyway I'm going for my tea now see you both"
"Yea ok Danny" Answers Pete.

Back at the nick Chief Super McClure, Inspector Hardy, Johnny and Ivor in the Chief's office the chief says
"I think he's lying and all the other kids will be lying for him but we'll take the statements from them anyway see to it Johnny, you and Ivor"
"Yes Sir will do" and left.

The following day at Mrs Longhurst's
"Here you are mum" Johnny bringing his mothers breakfast
"Thank you John"
"I heard the post I'll go pick it up probably circulars for the bin"
"Get your breakfast John I'll just see what it is" Johnny picks up the mail and walks through to the room
"Looks like a letter from our Frankie mum"
"O good read it John" Johnny opens the letter and says

"Our Frankie's coming home for a couple of days here mum I'll put it open on your table and I'll get my breakfast"
"Alright love" Jean says.

At the Laine's just having there breakfast Jill saying to Jim
"Our Danny took Jean to the shops yesterday didn't you Danny"
"Yes she enjoyed the shopping and fresh air" Jim says
"that's my boy good and helpful, that's what I want you to be a good clean lad like your brother Shaun"
"Yea ok dad" Danny resenting that, like Shaun.

At Mrs Longhurst's Johnny about to leave for work
"See you later mum"
"Ok John have a good day, I'll try mum" as Johnny opens the door Pauline just walking up to the door
"Whoops hello Johnny just going are you" Johnny replies
"I am bye Pauline"
"Bye Johnny" at the same time Danny just leaving for school walking up the road he sees Johnny
"Hiya Johnny"
"O hiya Danny mum says you were a perfect gentlemen yesterday, do you want a lift?"
"No thanks Johnny" Danny replies
"I'm meeting my girlfriend
"Ok then see you Danny"

"Yea Ok Johnny" Danny replies.

At the nick Johnny just arriving in the car inside the station at the Chief's office, there is Chief McClure, Inspector Hardy and Detective Jones, Johnny walks into the station and the desk Sargeant says
"Johnny you have to go to the Chiefs office as soon as you come in"
"Ok Sarg" Johnny answers walking to the Chiefs office knocks and enters
"Morning everybody"
"Morning Johnny" the Chief answers

"We have three statements you and Ivor received, the one from the girl Joyce Allison stating that Down's was with her and also the two lads Gerry Armstrong and Harry Pearse saying that they saw downs with this girl at near the time when Mr Ford and his son Jake was supposed to have been beaten up by Joe Downs well away from the incident I just know there lying" Inspector Hardy then says!

"This boy Down's his name has been mentioned in a statement from Mr Fords brother Billy Ford in a statement that he hit Joe Downs in self defence the three lads that was named at the scene at the incident was Danny Laine, Harry Pearse and Pete Lawson and none of them have been in to make a statement"

"I wonder why" Johnny says

"Danny Laine runs errands for my mother so I'll have a word with him Sir"

"Alright Johnny" answers the Inspector

"We'll just wait and see if any of them comes in"

At this time back at Mrs Longhurst's there's Pauline doing some house work when Jill Laine knocks and walks in

"Hello Jean, Pauline" Pauline answers

"Hiya Jill"

"I suppose you could smell the tea brewing" Jean says

"Did you Jill"

"I thought I could " then Jean says

"We've had a letter this morning Jill from our Frankie and he's coming home for a couple of days"

"That's nice for you Jean"

"Yes it is, the last time he wrote was about a month ago he had just bought an EX R.A.F launch in which he said he bought so he could go out fishing and sleep aboard instead of going to a guest house or hotel in Aberdeen when he had time off"

"Was Danny alright taking you shopping Jean" Jean answers

"He was very helpful like he always is Jill"

"As long as he was Jean" Jill answers

"You have a treasure their Jill"

"That's fine then Jean" Pauline comes through

"Tea up" Jill and Jean smile at each other.

School leaving and Danny walking down with Pete when Joe and Gerry joins them

"Hiya Danny" Joe shouts

"Yea what you got to tell me then Joe"

"Nothing" Joe answers

"Are you going down to the usual place tonight"

"Probably"

"See you there"

"Yea ok Joe" Joe and Gerry run off, Pete says to Danny

"Joe does things and he's not bothered who knows" Danny says

"It just shows you what an idiot he is as long as we don't join in with his stupidness" at this time Johnny stops and says

"Do you want a lift Danny if your going to see if my mother needs anything"

"Yea thanks a lot Johnny, see you later Pete"

"Alright Danny" Pete answers.

Danny gets in the car and Johnny drives off, he says

"Danny, you and couple of your mates was supposed to go and make a statement about the incident concerning Joe Downs and Billy Ford when Billy Ford hit Down's"

"The thing is Johnny I wasn't completely sure if Joe did go for Billy or not and I don't want to go to the police station and make a statement that I'm unsure of anything"

"Alright Danny" Johnny says

"What about the others?"

"I don't know" answers Danny

"I don't think they know what really happened"

"Fair enough Danny".

Later after tea the gathering of the clan down at the old derelict building about 15 lads and lasses Danny walks in with Diane, Pete and Jackie, Gerry says

"Hiya Danny Joe says he's going to smash all the windows of old man Dowse's house because of what he heard, that old man Dowse told Billy Ford "that he saw what happened and he's on Billy Ford's side" Danny says

Fury

"That's up to Joe what he does people should mind there own business and everything would be fine" then Joe walking down the road heading for Mr Dowse's house, he sees Jason, Jason says

"Hiya Joe where you going" then Joe tells Jason what had happened with Billy Ford and Mr Dowse was going to make a statement in favour of Billy Ford

"So I'm going to smash his fucking windows so he'll think again his old woman's got alzimers so if I hit her with a housebrick it might do him a favour" Both then starts laughing.

"Come on Joe I'll come with you"

"Ok Jason" walking down the road Joe saying to Jason

"When I've sorted old man Dowse out I've this address of an old woman that's still in hospital might be a good time to see what's in the house, fancy it Jason"

"Yea" Jason replies

"Why not nothing else to do" nearing Mr Dowse's house Joe says

"Let me find a brick or something" Jason says

"Make sure nobody's looking" Joe says!

"Fuck 'em if they are" Joe picks a brick up and going down Mr Dowse's yard, Jason stops near the gate Joe gets to the door and knocks, Mr Dowse comes to the window and says

"What do you want" Joe says

"Come and answer the fucking door it's ignorant when somebody knocks on your door and you don't answer, just to let you know this bricks coming through your fucking window and if you want to lie for Billy Ford you'll get more but only worse" At this time Joe lets fly at the window with the brick and smash's it then takes off with Jason, Jason says

"You don't give a fuck do you Joe!"

"No why should I, what can he do the silly old bastard" Joe answers.

At Mr Dowse's

"What's that noise Jack" says Mrs Dowse

"Nothing Doris it's just me banging about" Mrs Dowse answers

"Well don't!" Mr Dowse goes through to the kitchen talking to himself

"What will I do, should I do nothing and hope nobody comes back, I don't know, poor Doris most of the time she doesn't know what's happening anyway, maybe a good job I wouldn't want her life a hell, like these young kids do to people.

Joe and Jason nearing the old lady's bungalow that Joe robbed and hit, Joe looking at the purse with the address on
"Hey Jason, look this is the one, come on lets go in through the back" Joe and Jason go and smash the back window and get into the bungalow looking round going in to everything Jason in the living room and Joe in the bedroom going through the draws and wardrobe Joe comes across the lady's jewellery box with all kind of jewellery inside, Joe takes the lot then in the wardrobe a shoe box with papers and money, Joe shouts
"Jason come here look at this" Jason comes through and sees all this money in the shoe box, Joe says
"there must be a couple of thousand pounds here" Jason says
"Come on grab some put it in your pocket I'll do the same what else is there"
"only photos and things" Jason says
"Come on Joe lets go"
"Ok" Joe answers
"You get out and I'll follow" but before Joe goes out he sets fire to a few papers and kicks them all over setting fire to other things in the bungalow, Joe goes out he see's Jason on the pavement walking away from the bungalow Joe comes running out gets to Jason and says
"Come on Jason that fucking place will be going up in smoke in a few minutes" Jason says
"What you done" Joe says
"Flamed it" Jason says
"You silly cunt do you want to get caught!"

As they take off down the road a neighbour sees what looks like a fire in the old lady's bungalow gets on his mobile and phones for the fire brigade.

Back at the derelict building, Joe and Jason arrive

Fury

"Nobody else there" Joe says

"Lets count this money"

"Here" Jason emptying his pockets with cash and Joe doing the same, as they are counting it Danny comes, he says

"What you got there"

"Plenty of money what me and Jason got"

"Where from" Danny asks, Joe says

"From that old woman's bungalow the one we got her purse off"

"Here I'll help you count it" they count all the money of which they count £2,150 Danny then says

"What you going to do with it all" Joe says

"Thought me and Jason could have a thousand pound each and you can have £150 Danny, then Jason says

"What about all that jewellery you've got Joe"

"Yea, let me get it out, there's rings necklaces gold sovereigns and bracelets" Danny says

"Ok Joe I'll have the £150 and the sovereigns and don't say anything to anyone else about it because if you do, I don't know anything about it ok Jason"

"Yea that's fine Danny" Jason replies,

"Right I'm going now Danny says, you haven't seen me"

"Yea ok Danny" both Joe and Jason reply.

The fire brigade at this time putting out the fire at the old lady's bungalow with neighbours outside looking on! at Mr Dowse's house, on the phone trying to contact Billy Ford, he then gets an answer, Billy at the other end says

"Yes" Mr Dowse says

"Its me Billy Jack Dowse?"

"Yes Jack are you alright"

"No I'm not Billy I can't go to the police to make a statement about the incident that happened between you and that lad Downs"

"Why what's the matter Jack, Jack says

"He's been to my house and put a brick through the window and threatened more, I can't do with it, with Doris having alzimers I have enough to do with looking after her I'm sorry Billy"

"Why don't you contact the police and tell them everything"

"I can't take the chance, I'm sorry Billy" then puts the phone down, Billy left dumb foundered.

The following day at Mrs Longhursts a knock on the door it opens and Frankie comes in
"Hiya mum"
"O Frankie!" Mrs Longhurst shouts out
"O love its good to see you"
"Good to see you as well mum" Frankie goes up and cuddles his mum and kisses her
"How long are you going to stay love" Frankie says
"Just a couple of days, is our Johnny at work"
"Yes he is love put the kettle on Frankie and make a cup of tea and make yourself a sandwich there's some ham in the fridge I've got my cup and flask here Frankie I can make my own"
"No you don't mum I'll make you one"
"Alright love, what's new Frankie"
"I'll tell you mum I've done a little fishing on the boat and eaten some good fresh fish, the boat's the best thing I've ever bought I can just go where I want when I'm not working, in-fact mum I've brought some nice fresh haddock home for all of us"
"Oh that's nice our John will like that" Frankie walking through bringing the tea's form the kitchen, putting them down on Jean's table near her chair "I'll just get my sandwich"
"Alright love".

When at this time Johnny comes in from work "Hiya mum"
"Hey John there's someone in the kitchen to see you"
"Who?" Johnny replies then Frankie comes through "Hello Frankie"
"Hiya John good to see ya' mate"
"Ditto" Johnny replies "well then Frankie your going to have to tell us what you've been up to then, you play boys will have plenty to say" Frankie smiles ridiculously and says "I haven't been up to much"
"What!" Johnny shouts "all these dolly birds and parties on this boat of yours

Fury

"I wish!" Frankie whispers "I was thinking in about 3 or 4 months or so, when I've got the boat how I want it maybe you and mum can come! and we can arrange our holidays together, so just us three can enjoy going out on the boat! I'm going to have ramps put on in the right place so mum can be moved around without any problems! And then hopefully you never know we might get some sunshine how's that feel for both of you"

"That would be wonderful Frankie won't it John?"

"Yes it will be mum"

"Well that's it then all settled" Frankie says as he claps his hands and then cuddles his mum also he puts his arms around Johnny and say's I love you both we are a good family we are all start laughing and Jean crying a little with joy.

At the police station Billy Ford enters to the desk sergeant "yes sir can I help?"

"Yes my names Billy Ford I was brought in by both Pc Dent and Pc Taylor about an incident concerning myself and a lad who goes by the name of Joe Downs"

The desk sergeant says, "Yes I seem to remember you and that particular incident what can I help you with?"

"Well this old boy Jack Dowse saw the incident and he knows that this boy Downs attacked me he was coming to make a statement to confirm what he saw and now he isn't because he had a brick lobbed through his window by this piece of shit! because he's now frightened he has an ill wife and he doesn't want to get involved with anything! now can you send someone down to see him and have a chat with him it will not only clear me but it will get these arseholes off the streets" the desk sergeant says

"Look Mr Ford give me the gentlemen's address and I'll see what the inspector decides really unless we receive a complaint from Mr Dowse and a written statement I don't believe we can do much"

"Well then what is law biding people supposed to do? Put up with this kind of terrorising by the kind of under age dick heads"

"I'm sorry I can only say what is decided by the inspector"

"Yeah yeah yeah whatever in other words you let them do what they bloody like". As Billy is leaving he turns around and say's "there's one thing with the police they sure know how to look after the criminals and there brilliant with speed cameras there's that many get on there little arses with there little cameras there's not enough coppers to see the real criminals what we have here is the biggest part of the police force are overpaid traffic wardens anyway! and the rest looking for a big bust so it is on the front page of the paper what about other people I'd go and make a cup of tea sergeant" then Billy leaves. The sergeant goes to the inspector's office to tell him what has happened.

The next day at Mrs Longhurst's John and Frankie where having breakfast along with Jean as well "what will you be doing today Frankie?" asked his mother

"Well I'd thought I'd take you out for a run you know it's a lovely morning"

"Oh that'd be lovely Frankie! what time will you be coming home Johnny"

"Ermm about 5:30" replies Johnny

"Well that's alright mum we can have a good run out and we'll get some fish and chips as well how's that sound eh?" Jean with a hideous smile " that'll be great! that's settled then" at this time Pauline knocks and comes in the door "hello Jean, Johnny and Frankie"

"Hello Pauline" they answer, "After Frankie and I get ready with a little help from you Pauline Frankie and I are going out"

"Oh that'll be nice Jean," says Pauline "I'll have a tidy round for you and then I'll be off"

"We wont be going for an hour or so! so you don't have to rush Pauline," says Jean

"OK but I'll get started anyway," Pauline replies.

Then at the Laines just finished their breakfast Susan says, "Must go mum"

"Yep we'll see you later love," Jim says "I'll just finish the paper off Jill and I'll be away I have to be there to take the bus out in 40 minutes! was that our Danny I heard going out the back way love?"

"Yes he never even said see ya' well never mind eh?" Danny walking down the road to school meeting up with Diane "Hiya babe" Danny says to Diane "What are you doing tonight?" Diane says

"I don't know yet what do you want to do?"

"Well you know Di" Danny replies! grabbing her around the waist, walking further up the road and they see Joe, Harry and Gerry walking to school Joe turns and see's Danny! he shouts across the road "Hiya Danny what are you doing tonight?"

"I'm not sure yet" Diane shouts

"I know what he's doing he's seeing me for a change"

"Alright yea no problem Diane, just asking that's all" Joe says, Harry turns and says

"Ay Joe look at this kid on the bike from the Sunningdale School!"

"Yeah hit the idiot round his head" so as the lad is nearing Harry slaps him on his head then Joe Fists him on the head and the lad comes off his bike

"Get up you fucking idiot" Joe shouts laughing as he runs off with the rest of them, a man and a woman stops to help the lad up, he's got a cut hand and cuts on both his legs, the lady says

"Are you alright can you get up ok"

"Yes thank you" the boy about 11 years old said to them both, the man said

"Do you want us to phone the police or ambulance?"

"No" said the lad

"I'm alright now" and leaves getting on his bike.

Then down at Jack Dowse's a police car pulled up with Pc Peter Walker and Pc Harry George getting out and going towards Mr Dowse's door knocking when Jack Dowse opens it, Pc Walker says

"Mr Dowse" who answers

"Yes"

"We've just come to see you about a problem you've had about somcone smashing your windows, can we come in?"

"No" answers Jack

"I don't want to see you I have nothing to say" Pc George says

"Mr Ford has came to see us to say you saw what happened the other day concerning Mr Ford and some lads, with Mr Ford retaliating in self defence so Mr Ford says, but he always says you can verify the incident and since one of the youths has probably put your window through if you just tell us what you can we can help you"

"Help me!" Jack says

"The only thing that happens to these yobs is a slap on the wrists, the law says they can get away these things you've only got to look at the papers day in day out people getting beat up by gangs of youths mostly old people, when you see there photos in the paper with bruising and black eyes and that's just seventy plus year olds, some of their life savings are stolen in fact people live in terror against these yobs and until something or somebody decides to do something about it I'm not speaking to you or anybody, I'm sorry but I'm also sorry for people who have suffered and people who haven't suffered yet, but sure will in time" Jack says

"So goodbye!" and shuts the door, Peter and Harry look at each other, and Peter says

"He's right you know Harry" Harry says

"I know! what can we do?" they both walk down the path to the car and leave.

At the station, Susan Laine and Johnny passing each other near the desk

"Hiya Johnny"

"Hiya Susan how are you?" Johnny says

"I'm alright are you?"

"Yes thanks" Susan replies

"I see Frankie's home"

"Yea for a couple of days"

"Has he brought his lady friend with him?" Susan asks

"Lady friend, you've got to be joking, our Frankie I think he's to busy working if your not doing anything Susan why don't you ask him to take you out"

"Oh no I wouldn't do that he's come to see you and your mum"

"Look I'll have to go Susan Inspector Hardy wants to see me"

"Alright Johnny bye"

"Bye Susan" at Inspector Hardy's office!
"Johnny, the old lady that got badly beat up and robbed"
"Yes sir"
"She still in hospital?"
"Yes sir she is"
"Her bungalow has been robbed and set on fire"
"Any witnesses sir"
"None at all, the sooner we get police cameras the sooner the better it would help, but we daren't inform the lady because she's too poorly, we have informed her son about what has happened, I have sent two officers to make enquiries, I don't know if they will come up with anything or not"

"No sir that's a fact" Johnny replies. Reaching for some papers out of the desk reading them out

"One is Susan Laine's brother Daniel Laine, Joe Downs, Peter Lawson, Harry Pearse and Gerry Armstrong being the main names but at this stage we have nothing to bring them in for we will have to keep an eye on them when we can, it's obvious we haven't the man power to watch them all the time! we have got to hope when they make mistake's and seen by the public and hopefully the public will come and tell us, anyway Johnny get yourself off now I know you've got things to do" yes sir! then Johnny leaves

School leaving and Frankie on his way back home with his mother after there day out
"Nearly home mum should just about beat our Johnny home won't we"

At the Local Willy's store a gang of youth's just stood outside the doors with their use of baseball caps and hoods on, people walking by, one gentleman with a stoop back and walking stick walking by about six of the youth's they start walking behind him shouting abuse at him one lad shouting

"Go on you old bastard walk straight you silly old cunt" the old man trying to walk as fast as he can shouting

"Leave me alone I don't hurt anyone" still chanting at him when an elderly old lady say's to the boys

"Leave him alone the mans old enough to be your grandad would you like your grandad to have to put up with that" one of the lads say's

"Fuck off you old cow" just at that time Danny walks up with Joe Downs, Pete Lawson and Gerry Armstrong Joe takes some eggs out of the old lady's bag,and Danny say's

"Sling em at the old codger" at this time Joe's taking them out of the box and lets fly at the old man and hitting him on his back and throws the rest in the box at the old women a man comes out of the store and say's

"Leave the old people alone" as he say's that one of the yobs runs and smacks him in the face and then runs away

"Yes" the man say's

"That's all your good for hit and run and always in gangs aren't you brave bastards" Then a police siren coming down the road all the youths ran away. The police pull up Pc Dent and Pc Taylor get out of the car all the people complaining to the police officers the old lady and the old gentlemen looked very upset and frightened the man that came out of the store called Martin Jarus say's to the police officers

"Why isn't there anything positive done then about these youths" the two officers just looking in sympathy

"But I can recognise one of the pieces of shit the one that threw the eggs his name Is Joe Downs he lives where I used to live until last year down Lily-smith road" Pc Dent say's

"Can we just take a few notes to help bring some of these people in! can we just see you first love" to the old lady Pc Dent say's

"And my partner will speak to you sir" the old man with the walking stick.

Further down the road there's Danny, Joe, Pete and Gerry walking they bump into six-former Jimmy Hackett and a few of his mates Danny say's

"Hiya Jimmy" Jimmy just say's

"Downsey come here I want you"

"Yea what do you want Jimmy?"

"Don't fucking call me Jimmy you short faced piece of shit" Jimmy say's

"What about that lad you hit and knocked off his bike along with Harry Pearse"

"He called me a name" Joe say's

"Don't lie camel breath he wouldn't lie to anybody that's the difference between you and him"

"Why who's he supposed to be" Joe say's

Jimmy answers

"He's my young cousin he's eleven how old are you? You ugly bastard" Danny say's "Ok Jimmy you've made your point" Jimmy say's

"Keep your nose out of this one Laineee" Joe then say's

"Why what will you do about it with these supposed hardo's" Jimmy then grabs Joe and smacks him in the face two to three times Joe then covered in blood then down on his knee's screaming "You rotten bastard Hackett" Jimmy say's

"Rotten sometimes but I'm no bastard shut your mouth Downsey" and then Jimmy boots him in the mouth Danny then say's

"Leave him alone now Jimmy"

"I told you once keep your nose out of it or you can have the same Laine anyway you can tell your mate Harry Pearse he's got something to look forward to when I see him" Jimmy and his mates walk away leaving Danny and Co helping Joe up. Joe say's

"He's broke my fucking nose" Danny say's

"Come on Joe get yourself home"

Soon after Pc Dent and Pc Taylor coming down the road Pc Dent say's

"These look like who I think they are"

"Your right Roger" say's Pc Taylor they stop where the four lads are Roger gets out of the car and looks at Joe and say's

"Now then young Downs what number bus hit you then" Danny then say's

"He fell down at the top of the street"

"That right then Joe" Joe replies

"Yea" Pc Dent say's

"Do you feel alright then?" Joe say's

"How do you expect me to feel"

"I don't know" replies Roger

"Because your named by a witness that knows you about the trouble outside Willy's store concerning snatching someone's eggs out of an old lady's bag and throwing them at both an old man and lady you stole them from and then the abuse you gave with the rest of your mates, that includes you three as well" Danny said

"I was there but I didn't say or do anything" and the other two said

"And we didn't either, we was all coming home from school we had to pass near there"

"And that applies to me" Joe said, Roger then said

"Whether you did or not we know for a fact young Downsey did"

"Come on Downsey we'll take you home so your mother and father knows what's happened, Danny on his way home sees Harry Pearse

"Hiya Harry you wouldn't of heard but the kid you and Joe hit and knocked off his bike was Jimmy Hackett's cousin and he's beat Joe up and says he's going to do the same to you" Harry replies and says

"If that's what he thinks I am not frightened of Hackett" Danny says

"I'm pleased you think that way Harry at least you know so when you see him you can get the first one in"

"Yea I'll do that Danny see you"

"Yea ok Harry see you"

At Mrs Longhursts Frankie and Jean settle down to a cup of tea and Johnny walks in

"Hiya you two"

"Hiya John, we've had a lovely day out what a refreshing time, out for a ride in the country at the pub for a little drink and a bite to eat, it was great john"

"I've told mum Johnny you'll have to get a holiday week in! then as I said before we'll all have a week together, better for both of you"

"I'll see to that Frankie but in the mean time Susan Laine's been asking about you if you got a girlfriend or anybody I think she wants you to take her out why don't you ask her Frankie" Jean says

"She's a very nice girl"

"I don't know, I don't know what I'm going to do yet after all I'm only here a couple of days and I've really come too see mum and you Johnny"

"Ok Frankie just trying to do the girl a favour"

"O yeah" Frankie replies laughing.

The following day Harry Pearse with two young kids about 11 to 12 years old walking up the road as Jimmy Hackett walking towards them, Harry sees Jimmy as does Jimmy see Harry, Jimmy says

"Now then Pearsie what did you knock my young cousin off his bike and hit him for" Harry says

"It was an accident I just put my arm out as you do in a bit of fun it was Joe Downs that pushed him from his bike and hit him"

"Whether you say what happened with you was an accident, accident or not leave him alone because if you don't I'll come looking for you Pearsie and it wont be no accident then, because I'll knock your silly face in, get me!"

"Yeah sure Jimmy" Harry says, they then go there own ways as Harry's walking away with his two little kids he walks into Ricky North

"Hiya Rick haven't seen you in a few days" Harry says

"No me dad made me stay in for a while, how are you Harry"

"Ok" he answers they then go off altogether.

At the derelict building all the gangs just about here messing about, smoking shit, drinking cider and some of the kids climbing up onto the roof unsafe that it may be, as Harry and Ricky North arrived, a police car showed up almost all the kids except them on the roof run off, Harry and Ricky with the two kids that was with them, the two police officers Pc Dent and Taylor said

"Come on lads down off the roof" looking at Harry Ricky and the two kids Pc Taylor said

"What are you lot doing here then" Harry answers by saying

"We're just on our way home, we got here passing through the same time as you came" Pc Taylor said

"Ok you better get going then" so they did, he then shouted to the three on the roof and said

"Do you realise you could kill yourselves off the roof because its unsafe so I'm going to give you all a caution and that's if we catch you again, you will be summonsed"

"Alright" they all said

"Right you can get in the car and we'll take you home and let your parents know where you have been and that you have been cautioned" They all got into the police car and leave down Orial Street.

On her way to the shops is Mrs Ford, Jake Ford's mother heading towards a gang of young girls and boys and nearing them is Ricky North and Harry Pearse when Harry says

"Look Ricky over the road Jake Ford's old woman"

"Yea! hey girls give Jake Ford's mam some verbal shit" one of the girls about eleven years old says

"Ok" and only the girls start shouting at Mrs Ford

"Hey slag, you ugly pig come over here and we'll pull your stupid looking hair out" Mrs Ford just looks without saying anything, Harry says to the girls

"Go across and boot her" three of the little girls run over towards Mrs Ford, Mrs Ford looks and looks across the road and shouts

"Ricky tell them to stop" Ricky just looks and says nothing at the time when one of the girls kicks Mrs Ford on her leg another push's her over onto a near by car parked up another girl slaps her in the face at this time a man coming down the road, shouts

"Hey leave the woman alone" the girls run away so do the other kids at the other side of the road except for Ricky and Harry just looking on when a new kid on the block walks up to Ricky and Harry and says

"That was good to watch three little girls beating that silly cow over the road" Ricky says

"Who are you"

"My names Steve Bean just moved in down here in Orial Street" holding his hand out to Ricky and Harry, they shake hands

"Nice to meet you both" the man who goes to help Mrs Ford shouts across at the lads can you give me a hand with this lady, Harry shouts

"Fuck off you help her knob head" they then go, the man helps Mrs Ford up and says

"Should I phone the police" Mrs Ford says

"No that'll be a waste of time I didn't know them girls"

"Well will you be alright" he says

"Yes I'll be alright and thank-you for your help" she then carries on going to the corner shop, at the usual corner the baseball cap and hoodies gather, Ricky North, Harry Pearse and the new kid Steve Bean walks up to the gang, Danny is there along with Pete and Gerry Armstrong, Ricky says

"Danny a new lad just moved into the area, Steve Bean, this is our big mate Danny"

"Hiya Danny pleased to meet you"

"Yea ok where are you going"

"Nowhere answers Ricky but old lady Ford has just had a thumping from some of the eleven year old girls"

"What for" asks Danny

"What for!" Ricky says

"They tried to get me put in the nick for a while" shouting

"Don't shout at me Ricky" Danny says

"Otherwise I might just get annoyed with you" Ricky says

"Sorry Danny I didn't mean too! was you lot there" Danny ask's

"Yes" says Harry

"What did you do"

"Nothing" said Harry

"Did Mrs Ford see you there"

"Yes but we didn't have anything to do with them lasses getting her"

"Even so" Danny said

"You know you'll have old man Ford and his brother looking for somebody more likely for you two!".

The following day going to school Danny, Diane, Pete and Pete's girlfriend bumps into Ricky, Joe and the new kid Steve

"Hiya Danny" Ricky says

"Hiya Rick I didn't think you'd be at school today Joe! what happened with the law"

"They gave me a caution and said to stay out of trouble"

"That'll be hard for you to do won't it Joe" Danny says laughing carrying on down the road to school.

At Mrs Longhurst's just finishing breakfast, Johnny stands up from the table to get his jacket on

"I'll have to go now mum"

"Ok John look after yourself"

"I will" says Johnny

"See you later Frankie"

"Ok Johnny see you later" then Johnny leaves for work

"Right mum" Frankie says

"I'll just get rid of the pots and clean and put them away then if you like we'll have another run out because I'll be going back to the rigs tomorrow"

"Can't you stay another day or so Frankie"

"I can't mum I'm due to be back the day after tomorrow but it wont be long before you and our Johnny's coming up to stay with me for a week on the boat"

"Alright love" Jean says

"Now in that case lets get things together and we'll go for a run in that there car of mine" Jean laughing saying

"Right lets go then"

"That's it mum do like I tell yea" they then both start laughing.

At the Fords! John asks

"How are you Lillian today"

"Just a little bruised John I'm starting to get frightened to even go to the shops now when little kids about ten and eleven run up to you and kick you and push you over chant absurd names at you for no reason at all"

"You said Ricky North was across the street and you shouted for help from him and he just said nothing"

"Yes John he's not going to help with what's happened at court"

"Yea I know the coppers say to our Jake, tell us everything that happened at the bungalow and all you'll get is just burglary expecting a conditional discharge in which that's all that little bastard got for killing that old boy, we all told Jake to tell the truth of what happened"

"But because we did we've got to suffer this kind of thing, where's the police now John we wont suffer like this I'll see Billy and see what he says what's happening"

"Fuck the police there like my fucking arse hole! look when they took our Billy to the police station for hitting that little bastard Downs they'd have prosecuted him if them little pieces of shit had have gone and lied on statements who would they have believed; we know who they would have believed them fucking bastards" John then grabs Lillian and starts crying

"Come on John don't get upset"

"I'll finish up killing the bastards if they don't leave us alone"

"Come on John calm down you know your not that kind of person to do anything like that come on let me make you a cup of tea and I'll phone Billy up".

The kids start leaving school Danny and the rest of his mates walking home walking towards them is John and Billy Ford, Danny says

"Hey there's Jakes dad and his brother Billy Ford coming up I'm off come on Pete" Danny and Pete cross over the road to the other side leaving Ricky, Gerry, Harry, Joe, and the new kid Steve Bean and some little kids, as John and Billy approach the new kid on the scene says

"Come on lets beat'em up" Billy Ford heard! what he said! Billy says!

"What did you just say" Steve says

"Fuck off I wasn't talking to you" looking big and clever at Billy, Billy carried on walking towards him almost face to face with the big boy, Billy then head butts him the lad holding his face bleeding he then started crying he says

"What have you done that for I'm only fourteen" Billy then says

"Anymore want to try I understand you said lets go beat'em up meaning me and our kid it's a known fact you scum can't do it on your own can you looking at the rest of them" John says

"Come on Billy lets go" but Billy carries on

"Do you know if you lot was put in the army and they sent you to somewhere like Iraq you'd be the quickest fucking runners in the country with yellow shit running out your arses, not one of them said anything just stood looking the big boy on the floor crying Danny and Pete across the road looking then Joe Downs with his messy face says

"I don't want anymore trouble with you Billy not with your brother or Jake and I don't think any of us will do anything against you, well If you do"

"Let's carry on now! you fucking lot started all this" Joe says

"Honest Billy shake on it"

"Fuck off and keep out of my way and any of my family, start being clever bastards again not will you be fucking talking but you wont be fucking walking either understand what I'm telling you eh!" shouting it, Joe says

"Ok Billy" at this time a crowd had gathered and some people shouted

"Well done mate" Billy then says

"Fuck off and pick your BRAVE mate up your lots leaving first not me" so the lads then set off down the road Danny and Pete looking on at them they then cross the road to join them Danny said

"I think we should call it a day with the Fords that means you better not say anything to Jake either"

"We've decided that Danny!" Danny then says

"Come on Pete I'm going home to get my tea then I'm seeing Diane later on"

"Ok let's go" Pete answers.

At the Fords John and Billy just coming through the door Lillian greets them

"Anything happened" Billy says

"Don't worry no more Lillian because if them fucking idiots start again I'll see some of my mates and we'll go get the the fucking lot of em, aye I'm talking like them now saying we'll get em ay Lillian make us a cuppa" Billy say's.

At Mrs Longhurst's house just arriving back after the day out Frankie wheeling his mother back to the house, opening the door to go in when Danny comes up "Hiya Mrs Longhurts hiya Frankie" both Frankie and Jean answer

"Hello Daniel"

"Would you like anything from the shop or anything Mrs Longhurst"

"No but thank-you for coming to see Daniel"

"That's alright Mrs Longhurst see ya' tomorrow bye both of you"

"Yea! see ya' Danny" Frankie say's Danny goes and Frankie gets his mum in doors "Now then mum I'll make you a cuppa and then you can decide what you want for your tea!" Jean replies by saying

"Well we'll have bacon, egg and tomatoes something quick because John will be home soon"

"O-k then mum!" Frankie goes into the kitchen! and on the corner of the usual haunt for the scum! Most of the boys and girls are there! Doing their usual intimidation of people walking by! When Harry says, "Ay you should see what's just moved into our street this great big fat bloke! His stomach is nearly down to his knees and his wife looks like a witch"

"Have they got any kids?" Harry said

"Yes I think they have a lass and a lad"

"How old?" Gerry replies

"I don't know maybe the lads about 14 and the girl maybe about 16"

"We'll have to have a look at them tomorrow maybe". At this time Danny walks up "What's happening then?"

"Not much Danny" answers Harry "But Gerry's been telling us about this new neighbour down their street"

"Oh exiting eh?" Danny say's "See you all I'm going home for my tea!"

Then back at Mrs Longhurst's Jean, Johnny and Frankie having their tea,

"How's things been at work Johnny?" Frankie asks

"As usual remember that fire mum at the old factory"

"Yes I do John" answers Jean

"Well today at the youth court there where two 10 year-olds, one 11 year-old a 12 and a 13 year-old accused of arson I heard all five where in court crying, their solicitors said it was an accident and that they where just playing and they didn't mean to set it on fire they didn't realise the danger they just made a little camp fire! there solicitor said, as you can see they are deeply sorry of what happened and they have never been in trouble before for anything   and believes this has been a bad experience for such vulnerable young people and it has learned them a very big lesson of which he was certain that they will never get into trouble again the kids where still crying when they where all given a conditional discharge but then when they came out of court they where laughing and cheering what kind of law have we got"

"I honestly wish I knew! finish your tea John" Jean says "Don't get upset"

"Ok mum" Frankie puts his arm around Johnny

"any way I'll be away in the morning but don't forget you two will be coming up to me in a few weeks won't you?"

"We certainly will Frankie", answers Jean. The following morning Frankie just packing a few things in a case Johnny making Jean her breakfast Jean brushing her hair when a knock on the door! then opens it's Pauline

"Hiya everybody" she then comes in she says "Right where should I start come on boys you'll have to keep out of my way" smiling at Jean.

Outside on their way to school Danny, Diane, Pete and his girlfriend Jackie meeting up with the rest of the kids mainly Joe, Harry, Gerry and Steve Bean "Hey Steve you and Joe look like you've gone a round with Mike Tyson"

Of course they didn't answer just looking sorry for themselves"

Then Harry says "Hey are you going to come down and see our new neighbours later"

Danny says "Sure why not I need something exciting to happen tell some of them little kids to come as well your little pals Joe"

At the police station inspector Hardy see's p.c Dent and asks when is this guy coming in to make a statement about the incident at Willy's supermarket"

Fury

"I don't know sir" He said "He would come in and make a eye witness statement" answers P.c Dent when Johnny is walking through

"Johnny!" shouts inspector Hardy

"Yes sir" Johnny answers

"Come through to my office"

"Yes sir" getting into the inspectors office

"Sit down Johnny" as he does looking at the inspector as he says

"Do you know Johnny everyday we hear of complaints about these small band of young kids causing havoc, but we never get any real definite names and when we do we send them to court and what happens a big nothing! The tax payers pay their solicitors who get them off it seems that the time we put off trying to convict these people it's a complete waste of time I was thinking what that fella Billy Ford said the other day that some of the police are just over paid traffic wardens! I read the paper and in the paper the other day of how much the police make in speeding fines with the cameras! literally millions of pounds what annoys me is that criminals pay for nothing they even get there solicitors free! John you and me have been friends for a very long time now! so I wanted you to be the first one to know I am resigning from the force"

"But sir" Johnny says "What about your pension"

"What about it Johnny I was one of the brigade coppers when law, was law and there was respect for the law, and there was respect to one another but the more handfuls of shit heads grow more and more each week. And the same shitty laws stay in place, O-k it looks good headlines when we have a big drugs bust I know we have to get these people who supply drugs and give them lengthy jail sentences but we have to get the scum that terrorise, intimidate, assault and burgle people if they do the crime they should serve the time, name and shame the young kids and prosecute their parents! they can't be named! named for legal reasons in other words their under age! Then their parents are responsible for their behaviour they should be made to learn them right from wrong, the politicians make laws for the lawless, parents are told you can't smack em' otherwise their in trouble themselves the criminals know the law that's on their side. I can only see that things will get worse, before time the good law bidding people will have had enough and will finish having vigilante groups one day and who could blame them the police will have to look after the scum and hunt for the law bidding people I can't stay in the force to be a nurse maid to the pieces of shit! No Johnny I have thought about what will happen in due time and I'm finishing now! before I had told you I informed the chief and I'm not going to change my mind"

Johnny says, "I'm sorry to hear that sir but I do understand what you are saying"

Back at Mrs Longhhurst's Frankie now ready for leaving to go back to Aberdeen. Leaning over cuddles his mum and kisses her "See ya soon mum" Jean having a little cry and holding Frankie's hand and saying "Be careful as you go son I love you" Jean says

"I love you as well mum" Frankie then leaves,Jean sits back in her wheel chair to have a little weep.

School leaving at teatime there's Ricky, Joe, Harry, Gerry, Pete and Danny with Steve Bean running up behind them Danny says "Are we meeting at the corner later?"

"Yes" says all of them! Danny says

"Joe don't forget to get your little mates we'll go and see Harry's new neighbours"

Harry's new neighbours are a quite couple with two children a boy 14 and a girl aged 17, Brenda and Jimmy Jackson, Jimmy being not a well man having diabetes, liver and kidney complaints can hardly walk at all being very much overweight due to other complaints with his health he is a very placid man but having to move council houses because of his needs! this house has a lift in from the front room directly up into the bedroom which is ideal for him at least he will be able to go to bed at night rather than sit in the chair in the room and sleep in it at night like he had to in the other house, things seem to be alright now Brenda doing the best she can having to do practically everything, their two children the boy called James and the girl called Penny both being good kids and always trying to help in the home, they are having tea at their usual time at about six thirty, after Jimmy had taken all of his medication including his insulin when a brick comes flying through their window in which it made them all jump, Brenda gets up from the table very quick and goes to the front door and opens it to look out

Fury

to what is happening, she sees a gang of kids rough ages where between nine and eleven years old, she says

"What are you doing and who smashed our window!" when one of the kids throws a stone and smashes another window then they all run away chanting

"You witch".

A little up the road stands Joe Harry Gerry Steve Pete and Danny, Joe says

"What about that Danny they'll know that were here now let them shit themselves" Joe laughing when Danny leaves.

Brenda phones the police and then the council to say what the kids had done.

Then back at Mrs Longhurst's and Danny knocks, opens the door and goes in

"Hello Mrs Longhurst"

"Hello Daniel" Jean answers

"Would you like anything doing or anything from the shops"

"No thank you Daniel" Jean looking a little bit upset

"Everything alright Mrs Longhurst" asks Danny

"Yes I'm alright just a little bit upset with our Frankie going back to Scotland" Danny then goes to Jean and puts his arms round her and kisses her on the cheek

"Don't be upset Mrs Longhurst school breaks up for the holidays next week so I'll be able to take you out down to the shops or anything" Jean says

"Thank you Daniel you're a lovely good boy"

"That's ok Mrs Longhurst see you tomorrow"

"Alright Daniel" almost at the same time Johnny comes in

"Hiya mum"

"Hello John I'm pleased your home I've been a little bit weepy since Frankie left"

"That's alright mum we'll be going through to him in about 4 weeks wont we"

"Yes your right John answers Jean".

The following day at Brenda's and Jimmy Jackson's the council putting boards up at the windows that had been smashed all except the door and just one of the front windows until they got some glass to put back in, the council worker man said to Mrs Jackson

"That's it love probably be back tomorrow when we get the glass! has the police been to see you"

"No they haven't yet"

"Alright love hopefully see you tomorrow" then Brenda goes in she looks at Jimmy and says

"Are you alright love" Jimmy replies by saying

"No I'm not we've only been here three days and this happens I wish we had stayed where we was at least we knew everybody and it was quite a nice place no trouble like this" Brenda goes and cuddles Jimmy.

Where at the police station there are news paper reporters after hearing that Inspector John Hardy had put his resignation in, he explained why but more diplomatic! Chief super McClure comes through

"John" he says

"Can I see you please" and looking at the reporters

"That's all gentleman thank you, a further statement will be made later concerning the same"

"John" the chief says

"Why don't you give it a second thought"

"I've give it a lot of thought sir but I will not change my mind, thank you for your support sir and you will always be, I hope a good friend"

"Oh course I will John" answers the chief

"But what will you do"

"I think I might get maybe a job with some security company or something in those lines"

"I can only say when the time comes when you leave that I wish you and your family the best in the world John"

"Thank you Sir I think I better get back to work now sir"

"Right carry on John".

Fury

Later there was a gathering of the clan on the corner of the street there's the usual there when some little kids come up who was outside the Jackson's throwing bricks and stones last night, one little kid Shane says

"Hiya Joe where going down to that house again like last night"

"Yeah you do that! give them shit"

"Ok Joe" said the lad

"Then we can join you then Joe and be in a gang like yours"

"Yea go for it then" and the little kids left, walking down the road there's about ten of them putting two fingers up to the motorists and some pretend there going to run across the road and make the traffic swerve and slow down almost to a stop the kids just look and laugh heading towards lime tree street not far from where the Jackson's live coming up to near there house Shaun says

"Hey look they've boarded all their windows up except that one we missed last night, we'll get that one and some of them upstairs" the kids walking on the opposite side of the road having picked up some stones on there way start throwing them hitting the downstairs window and hitting two of the windows upstairs unfortunately on his own Jimmy is sat on the easy chair in the room with a stone that come's through just missing his head, outside his daughter Penny just coming home with her boyfriend Paul they both shout

"Hey"

"What you doing you idiots" shouts Paul and the kids run away, Penny and Paul run into the house

"Are you alright dad"

"Yea a stone just missed me that came flying through the window"

"Where's mum" Penny asks

"She's gone to the shop" says Jimmy

"Pass me the phone Penny, let me phone the police and the council we'll need the window blocked off and anymore if they have broken upstairs"

Outside Harry just going home and see's the damage that has been done by the little kids he says

"Bloody hell what a mess" and carries on walking home passing people who are looking stood near there gates, Brenda then just coming from the shop she sees what has happened and says to some of the people

"Anybody know what's happened and who's done it" some of them said

"No we just heared a noise"

"I know probably them little bastards that broke our other windows" and Brenda then goes into the house

"Are you alright Jimmy" Brenda asks! Penny says

"No he isn't a stone just missed him! me and Paul saw them kids do it they then ran off when we shouted, dads phoned the police and the council to block the windows that's been broken Jimmy just sat there looking Brenda says

"How are you Jimmy"

"I feel sick, what have we done Brenda, what have we done wrong" looking very sad and upset

"What have we come to" Brenda looking concerned at Jimmy and goes and puts her arms around him Jimmy just says

"What have we done to deserve this" Jimmy getting a bit stressed

"Penny go put the kettle on and make a cup of tea pet" Penny says

"Ok mum"

"Do you want me to do anything for you Mrs Jackson" asks Paul

"No love just keep watching incase the little shits come back" at this time a police car pulls up outside a policeman gets out and walks up the path to the house Paul opens the door and the policeman enters I am Pc Kenny Johnson he takes his hat off and says

"Is everybody alright"

"Aswell as we can be" Brenda says

"We have phoned the police twice because its twice we've had our windows put in, can you explain why they didn't send anybody the first time" the officer says

"I don't know anything about that I was out to see you now that you have had trouble with some kids throwing stones"

"Yes we have" answers Brenda

Fury

"We've only moved in just three days ago and look at the place now I have a poorly husband that is getting very stressed all this done by little kids about nine or ten years old"

"Where did you move from" asked the Pc

"From Laurel Grove"

"That's a nice quiet area what made you move here" says the Pc

"Because of the lift for my husband so he could go to bed at night and not sleep on the chair" answers Brenda, the constable says

"If I was you I'd ask the council to move you back" Jimmy then says

"Thanks for your advice constable we'd just like the culprits to be caught and dealt with"

"I'm sorry," the Pc said

"I didn't mean anything by what I said I'll just take a statement from you then see what we can do! then before leaving the officer said

"I'm ever so sorry for you all" looking deeply sorry.

At Mrs Longhurst's where Jean and Jill having a little chat Jill says

"There's one thing Jean your Frankie looks well"

"Yes he does Jill, I think if he had been here for a few more days he was going to ask your Susan out"

"Our John had been talking to Susan at work"

"I sometimes wish our Susan would find a nice fella to take her out because she just stays in after work, either watching TV, washing her hair or on the computer"

"She's a pretty girl I'm sure one day she will know when she finds the right person like I did with John and Frankie's father, you know Jill our Frankie is very much like his father when I see our Frankie I see my Frank" Jean gets a little weepy then

"Hey come on Jean" Jill says

"You'll soon be seeing your Frankie again soon and your Johnny will be home soon so I'll make a cup of tea for you both you and your Johnny and then I'll get back home Jim wont be long now"

"Thank you Jill you're a good friend" says Jean

"What are friends for Jean" answers Jill when Johnny comes in

"Hiya mum"

"Hello John, Jill's just making a cup of tea and for tea stew and dumplings what Pauline did before she left its on a low light on the cooker so you wont have to do any cooking John tonight"

"That's good of Pauline mum" says Johnny, Jean then says

"It sure is partner" and they both have a laugh, Jill comes through into the room

"There you are Jean cuppa for you and Johnny, now I'm going Jean so I'll see you tomorrow"

"Alright Jill" Jean says

"See you Jill, bye"

"Bye Jean" then John comes through

"There you are mum eat it all up like a good girl now"

"Thank you John" Jean says, eating their tea Jean says

"How's your day gone John"

"Alright mum except Inspector Hardy has resigned"

"What ever for John"

"He's fed up with things and the system as a whole and I can understand him, anyway mum come on eat that lovely stew"

"I will love, I will".

At Jim and Jill Laine's home Jill walks in, sees Jim

"Hello Jim"

"Hiya love" Jim answers

"Tea's in the oven a nice steak and potato pie followed by apple pie and custard"

"Can't wait" Jim says

"I'll just get washed and changed is our Danny in"

"No not yet love" Jill replies

"Only there's this new couple down lime road only been in a few days and they've had there windows smashed by little kids twice, Jack who lives down there said he saw these little kids running away and a bit further up the road was our Danny and some of his mates, he says we probably find more out from Danny when he comes in"

"Maybe" answers Jill

"Yea" Jim says

Fury

"Apparently the bloke who lives there is a very poorly man, what's becoming of kids today, things to easy for them I suppose" Jill then says

"Remember Jim there's more good kids in this world than bad ones"

"Yea I know that love" answers Jim

"They should take a leaf out of our Danny's book, if he was like that I'd disown him"

"Yea well he's not is he" answers Jill

"No he's not love" Said Jim

"How many kids would put themselves out like our Danny does, when he goes to Jean's to ask if she wants anything doing and taking her out in her wheelchair"

"Only the good kids" shouts Jim from the bathroom, at this time Susan and Danny come in the house together

"Hiya" they both say

"Hello loves" Jill replies it sounds like your dads just finished in the bathroom so you to can take it in turns to go Danny says

"You can go first Susan"

"Well thank you Danny I will" answers Susan when Jim comes in the room

"Hiya Danny"

"Hiya dad"

"Danny you and some of your mates were down lime road at the same time some little kids was throwing stones at a window at a house where a very ill man lives with his family, did you see who they were son"

"No I don't know who they were, little kids about nine or ten year olds can't remember seeing them before we were just walking down to Harry's he lives down there dad! when we saw what was happening the kids then ran off" Jill then comes through and says

"Come on Jim Susan's coming Danny go and wash your hands the tea is out" later after his tea Danny goes out to see his mates! walking down he sees Diane

"Hiya Danny where have you been I haven't seen you, and you haven't been round"

"I've been round and about" Danny says

"You must have just missed me what ever, anyway I'm walking down to the corner are you coming"

"Alright" Diane answers.

The day after at the police station a guy walks in to the desk sergeant and says

"I am James Stone" quite a stocky person and tall

"I've come to see if anything has been done about the assault on my mother Glady's Stone who is still in hospital and has had her home robbed and burnt can you tell me what is happening"

"The only thing I can say sir" says the Sergeant

"Things are still being investigated I can't tell you anymore than that"

"Well I see" says Mr Stone

"If ever I find out who is responsible with what has happened to my mother I will personally bust there knees and that's a fact"

"I'm sorry sir I can understand what you are saying but you cannot take the law into your own hands otherwise you will be in trouble"

"In that case you find them first and protect them because myself and my two sons are going to make enquiries can I ask you a question Sergeant what would you do if it was your mother" the Sergeant did not answer

"Good day Sergeant"

"Good day sir" answers the Sergeant at this time Pc Kenny Johnson arrives at the desk

"Good morning Sergeant"

"Hello Kenny" answers the Sergeant

"Sarg, I put my report in about the house down Lime Street that's had there windows smashed the past two days at Mr and Mrs Jackson's, the man's very poorly Sarg, I can honestly say I really feel sorry for them you can see they haven't got much and the man's really stressed out" the Sergeant says

"Until we know who is doing it there isn't a thing we can do about it we are getting in loads of things like this everyday not only that we can't cope we haven't the man power to see to things and cope from one end of the country to the other end they must be hundreds upon hundreds everyday of things like this happening and until things change things will only get worse if things don't change the only consolation there is, is that these arseholes today have got worse to come as years go by then if they reach old age they should think what they did to people for no reason and what they did to make people's lives a misery they have worse to come! Kenny lad that will be a fact".

Later on in the early evening James Stone and his two sons who are both on leave from the marines going to his mothers burnt bungalow, James sees some of his mothers neighbours he walks up and asks an old lady and gent Mr and Mrs Peter Jenkins! James says!

"What can you tell me, if anything at all, if anybody saw anything no matter how small we want to find the people responsible for what happened to my mother who is in a very poorly condition whatever anyone can tell us only goes as far as me and my two sons because who ever did this to my mother, one thing is they will have also done the second so please ask some of the neighbours to help me because remember it could have been you, please" James says

"Please help us" one old guy walks up and says

"Look son nobody dare say anything or give names no matter how upset we feel about poor old Gladys, and we all feel for her for what she had to go through if we give names and go to court against these young hoodlums not only will they get away with it in court they'll know who we are then it will be our turn"

"I swear on my mothers life" James says

"If we can get names it wont even go to court, look I'll leave my phone number and then if anybody knows anything they can contact me".

The following morning at Mrs Longhursts just finishing breakfast when a knock on the door and enters Danny

"Hiya Mrs Longhurst, hiya Johnny" they both answer Danny with a good morning

"Just popped in Mrs Longhurst to tell you we break up for the summer term today and if you like I can take you out in the wheelchair to the shops if you like Mrs Longhurst tomorrow"

"Yes that would be nice Daniel wont it John"

"Yes it will mum" replies Johnny

"Ok I won't see you then until tomorrow what time would you like to go out"

"I think about ten thirty will be alright Daniel"

"Ok Mrs Longhurst see you"

"Yes alright Daniel see you" Danny then leaves, Danny walking up the road he runs into Diane"

"Haven't seen you Danny" says Diane

"Well I've had things to do"

"Will I see you tonight"

"I've got to look after the baby mum and dads going out" Danny says

"In that case I'll be round at about eight o clock alright"

"Yes sure Danny" answers Diane.

Further along he sees Joe, Steve, and Ricky, Joe says

"Eh Danny going down Lime street to Harry's later after school to have a bit of fun are you coming" Danny answers

"Probably"

"See you later then Danny"

"Yea! ok Joe"

"See you Danny" Steve Bean says

"Yea! ok Steve see you as well Ricky" Ricky says

"I can't I've got to go home" Danny then says

"Have you been a naughty boy" laughing

"The old man says I've got to start doing some useful things he's bought me a computer to try help me learn something so I have to try"

"Ok Ricky do as daddy says eh lads" Danny says, Joe then says

"Yea don't have any fun".

Then at James Stones home he shouts his two sons

"I've had a phone call from a fella he wouldn't give his name but he says I am giving you two names who the two boys were one called Joe Downs and the other Jason Anderson they were the ones he saw coming down mothers path and he says they were definitely the two and then he hung up" James says

"At least we know who they are now" James's two sons Ronny and Jim says

"We'll find them dad leave it with us we'll know what to do then".

Down at Brenda and Jimmy Jackson's the council men that was there says

"We have been told to board the windows that are smashed and put just one window in so you have at least some light coming in" Brenda says

"Brilliant isn't it no windows except one"

"I'm sorry love but we can only do what we have been told to do I'm very sorry" says the council worker

"What a way we are supposed to live" says Brenda! Jimmy shouts

"Come in love, Brenda come in"

"Are you alright Jimmy"

"No I'm not I'm sick and fed up with these carrying on's" He then starts crying Brenda then goes to him and puts her arm round him

"Jimmy come on love I'll go down to the council officers and see what they can do we can't keep putting up with this the police don't seem to care let me see if we can't be moved with or without a lift upstairs we will just have to have a bed downstairs look our Penny is just coming in! I'll go now our Pennys here with you" Brenda says!

"Alright love answers Jimmy ".

Then up at the council office explaining things to a young woman Miss Julie Smethurst, Miss Smethurst says

"Would you fill these forms in Mrs Jackson then I'll pass them over to the housing officer he will then be in touch with you" Brenda says

"How long do you think it will be"

"I can't really say Mrs Jackson it normally takes two to three days for anyone to receive a reply in some cases a little longer it depends on the needs of the people"

"Look love our house from the outside looks like a war zone and my husband is getting very depressed" says Brenda

"I'm sorry Mrs Jackson I can only do what is laid down by the council procedure for me to do, I'm sorry" Miss Smethurst says! then Brenda leaves.

At Mrs Longhursts Pauline the cleaner just leaving as Jill comes in Pauline says

"Too late for a cuppa Jill but the kettle's still hot, bye everybody"

"Bye Pauline" both Jean and Jill answer

"Get yourself a drink Jill"

"Will do Jean".

Brenda Jackson arriving home Jimmy says

"What did they say Brenda" Brenda replies by saying

"They will attend to it as soon as possible and move us out somewhere else" Jimmy says

"I hope its somewhere like we had before! we never had any trouble there with people like these pieces of rubbish because at the moment Brenda I feel ill my hole body inside me feels like its turning over all the time" Then Brenda puts her arms round Jimmy to reassure him

"Things will soon be alright Jimmy"

"I hope so Brenda, I hope so! I cant live like this knowing I cant do anything myself to stop it, I am helpless".

Back at Mrs Longhurst's Jean and Jill having a chit chat Jean says

"Your Daniel called in this morning before going to school and says he will come and take me to the shops in the wheelchair tomorrow isn't he a good boy"

"He is Jean" answers Jill

"Its just that some of the kids he knocks around with, if he keeps palling around with these kids like them I can see him one day getting into trouble even though he seems strong will I think he can be easily led Jean"

"I don't know about that Jill he's to nice of a boy to get into trouble" Jill replies and says

"I hope your right Jean".

School now leaving early because of the summer holidays all the kids leaving walking and running down the street some chanting at people walking by minding there own business, and also you can see Danny and Diane walking down and running up behind there's Joe, Harry, and Steve Bean Joe shouts!

Fury

"Hang on Danny we want to see you"

"Yea what do you want" Danny says

"The young kids are going down Lime Street to cause agro again are you coming Danny"

"Don't think so I'm going home for my tea then I'm seeing Diane"

"You'll miss all the fun Danny" Steve says, he then says

"Come on Joe Harry lets go, see you Danny"

"Yea ok" Danny replies as Joe Harry and Steve are running down to there usual corner the little kids are waiting Joe says now Shaun are you going to see how many windows are left in" in a clever way

"See if you can hit the lot" laughing

"Yea we will Joe"

"We'll get going and we'll watch what a good job you do" all laughing they set off to Lime Street were Harry lives the young kids acting big and clever trying to be like the other three idiots as they are, on there way one little kid picks a stone up and lets fly with it at an oncoming bus it goes straight at the window next to the drivers window and shatters it, the driver stops near Joe Harry and Steve who is walking well behind the little kids! the driver gets out and its Jim Laine Dannys dad

"Ho aren't you Harry Pearse"

"Yes Mr Laine" answers Harry

"do you know who them kids was"

"No Mr Laine we was too far away to see"

"Right alright" Jim then takes his phone out and rings the depot to say what had happened then as the kids nearing Brenda and Jimmy Jackson's house Shaun says

"Look there's only one window downstairs that's in everybody aim at just that one and run" At that time they throw stones at the one window, some stones hitting the boards but some then hitting and smashing the window in the house, Brenda and Jimmy sat talking with Penny and Penny's boyfriend Paul, Paul runs to the door opens it and runs after the kids at this stage Jimmy is in a very bad state he is shaking and just looking up at the ceiling Brenda says

"Jimmy are you alright" Jimmy does not answer just shaking and staring Brenda says Penny come here to your dad while I phone for an ambulance and the police" Penny goes to her father and holds his hand Brenda phone's! she says I need an ambulance now,my husband seems to be in shock and he is a very poorly man with all sorts of complaints he needs help fast" the guy at the other end of the phone says

"There will be an ambulance on its way"

"Thank you" says Brenda the man asks to give him all details so that the nursing staff knows precisely what has happened Brenda explains everything to the man when Paul comes in he says

"I didn't catch anybody they scattered all over the place, how is your dad Penny"

"Not good as you can see my mums phoned an ambulance its on its way" at that time they could hear the ambulance siren coming down the road the ambulance pulls up and two medics get out and go to the door at the time Paul opens the door for the medics they enter and go straight to Jimmy they ask

"Has he been breathing alright" Brenda says

"He's just been like that shaking and staring at the ceiling saying nothing" one of the medics say

"We'll bring a chair in and take him to hospital he does need help I'll contact the hospital to let them know after we get into the ambulance" Brenda says

"Will it be alright to go with him" the medics say

"Of course it will we'll just get him first" they put Jimmy into the chair and head up the path to the ambulance lots of people are out looking to see what is going on the medics use there back lift to get Jimmy onto the ambulance Brenda says

"Penny you and Paul stay in until I contact you to let you know what is happening" Penny says

"Ok mum" Brenda then gets in the ambulance and leaves with siren and flashing lights Penny then looks at some of the neighbours and shouts

"Who is them kids what's been doing this some of you must know something and seen the kids and who some of them are she then starts crying

"Look what the little bastards have done to my dad" Paul puts his arms round her and says

Fury

"Come in Penny and we'll tidy all the glass up for your mum and dad and put something up against the window" they then walk in the house they just close the door when James comes in

"They've been smashing the other window I see! where's mum and dad" Penny explains to James what had happened, James then starts crying and says

"What's the matter with dad I want to go to him" Penny then says

"Wait until mum phones and we'll know what's wrong, come here James" then Penny puts her arms around him and Paul puts his arms around both of them at this time Penny starts crying also James crying and saying

"I want my dad, I want him home", outside from a distance Joe Harry and Steve start walking down towards Harry's home some people still outside talking to each other Joe says to the other two

"Hey the little kids done a right good job eh!" Steve says

"Yea couldn't have done better" Harry then says

"Shut up going by the neighbours now" one of the neighbours says

"Hey Harry did you see who any of them kids were"

"No I don't Mr Johnson we were to far away and it happened so fast then they started running away" Joe then starts laughing, as the three continue to walk to Harry's.

At Jim and Jill Laine's Jim comes in the back door

"Hiya love" Jill says

"Hello love" Jim replies

"You'll never believe this going down Lime Street in the bus some young kids throws a stone and shatters my front left hand side window they couldn't be more than eleven years old"

"Oh love" Jill says

"Where I stopped, there were some of Danny's mates walking down, I asked them if they knew who they was and they said no they were too far away"

"Do you think they did know them Jim"

"I don't know love but I'll ask our Danny if he can find anything out".

The following morning at Mrs Longhurst's Johnny has gone to work and Pauline helping Jean to get ready to go out shopping with Danny

"There you are Jean nearly ready just need to brush your hair" Pauline says,

"Oh thank you Pauline you're an angel" replies Jean when a knock on the door and enters Danny

"Hello Mrs Longhurst am I on time"

"Spot on Daniel he is a good boy this lad Pauline"

"Yes I know you keep saying Jean" answers Pauline

"Well I'll leave you two it now I'm going now I'll see you Monday"

"Alright pet" answers Jean

"Well Daniel if you can just help me get into the wheelchair we can go"

"Alright Mrs Longhurst and I'd like to say you look really bright today"

"Oh thank you Daniel you're a nice young gentlemen" and away Jean and Danny go after locking the door, Danny walking along the road with Jean and sees Joe and Gerry coming along on their bikes Joe shouts

"Hiya Danny" Danny looks and says

"I want to see you two later"

"What for"

"I'll see you later I'm taking Mrs Longhurst to the shops right now" Danny answers

"Yes ok Danny" both the lads reply

"See you later".

Then at James Stone's flat his two sons Ronny and Jim come in they both say

"Hiya dad" James answers

"Hiya lads" Ronny says

"We know who these two louts are and roughly where they go and where they live, we'll think things over dad from when we are on leave next time that will just be over two weeks"

"We'll get things right! alright lads"

Fury

"We are going to do this for nan and you also dad and ourselves"
"Ok lads" James says.

Down at the Jackson's there's Brenda, Penny, James, and Paul sat round talking
"At this time your dad" Brenda looking at James and Penny
"Is no worse which is good news I'll be going to see him in about half an hour I want you all to stay in incase the council workman come to repair the windows"
"Alright"
"Will you stay with them Paul"
"Yes Mrs Jackson I was going to anyway" answers Paul
"Alright love I'll just have a wash and get changed"

At this time Danny is taking Jean window shopping looking in a clothes shop window when a lady walking by says
"Hello Jean" Jean looks and says
"Hello Francine how nice to see you"
"How nice to see you Jean and looking so well and looking very good" Francine says
"Its nice to be out! its very nice to be out and I wouldn't be if it wasn't for this lovely young boy Daniel he is one of my friends son Jill Laine is his mother" Jean says
"Jill Laine, that's Jill Turner before she married isn't it Jean"
"Yes that's right" Jean answers
"How is she"
"Alright isn't she Daniel"
"Yes she is Mrs Longhurst"
"Well that's nice anyway Jean I hope I see you again soon and give my regards to your mother Daniel"
"I will" says Danny,
"Bye Jean"
"Bye Francine"
"Bye young Daniel"
"Bye" Danny answers
"Oh Daniel" Jean says

"Its nice to come out and see people you haven't seen for a year or two" Jean smiling as Danny pushing her along.

Down at the corner where the scumbags gather there, there are as usual Joe Gerry Harry and company! when the young kids with Shaun come up! there is about twenty five of them altogether Shaun says
"Hey there's no windows in the house near where Harry lives now"
"Yea I know Shaun and the bloke's in hospital as well"
"Yea fucking good eh" Shaun says, Harry then says
"Yes you've made your point but who shattered the window on that bus that was coming down the road before you smashed the windows on the house" Shaun says
"Me, good eh"
"Not so good because the driver of the bus was Danny Laine's dad and I'm sure he will knock your fucking head off when he finds out"
"Or no! don't tell him it was me, please Harry" says Shaun!
"I'll tell him if he asks, and I just know he will ask" Harry answers
"I didn't know it was Danny's dad I wouldn't have done it" says Shaun, Harry then says
"You better grovel Shaun I wouldn't like to be you" when one of Shaun's mates says
"Shall we go down park road to the pension bungalows"
"Yea come on lets go" At the time Danny's girlfriend walks up and says
"Does anybody know where Danny is"
"He's taking Mrs Longhurst out in her wheelchair"
"Sometimes I think he thinks more of an old woman than he does me".

Then at the Jackson's the phone rings Penny answers the phone and its Brenda at the other end Brenda says
"Get ready and phone a taxi and come to the hospital your dads not too well"
"Ok mum we'll be there as soon as possible"
"Alright love" Brenda says

Fury

"Dads in intensive care see you soon" Penny then phones for a taxi, James says

"What's up Penny its dad isn't it" While Penny's trying to get a taxi James starts crying

"Its me dad Paul I know it is he's worse" Paul says

"It might not be James" when Paul stands up and puts his arms round him, Penny gets through to a taxi firm and asks them to send a taxi urgently, she comes off the phone and says

"Come on James dry your eyes where going to see dad"

"What's wrong Penny" James asks?

"Nothing mum just said to come up to the hospital to see dad a taxi will be here soon Paul we'll go outside to wait for it will you lock up Paul"

"Sure love" Paul answers, Penny and James leave the house as Paul locks up at this time Shaun and his young band and shit heads are walking down the road near the Jackson's on the opposite side of the road when Paul looks across Paul shouts

"I recognise you little shit heads" looking across at Shaun

"I'll have you" Shaun throws a stone and shouts

"Fuck off" at this time the taxi pulls up and Penny, James and Paul get in, on the way to the hospital, Shaun and the kids give some finger signs.

At Mrs Longhurst's Danny and Jean getting back from there outing Danny unlocks and opens the door then wheels Mrs Longhurst in and closes the door afterwards Mrs Longhurst says

"Do you know Daniel I have enjoyed my day out I think you are a little darling and caring young person"

"That's alright Mrs Longhurst I enjoy taking you out I feel proud being with you and doing what I can do to help "answers Danny Jean then says

"Will you put the kettle on and make me a cup of tea" Danny walks through to the kitchen and puts the kettle on he comes back and says

"I've done that for you Mrs Longhurst anything else"

"Can you just help me off with my coat" in which he does and doing so he touches Jeans breast

"Sorry Mrs Longhurst" Danny says

"Alright Daniel just an accident" Danny then goes into the kitchen to make a cup of tea for Jean at this time Johnny comes in from work

"Hiya mum"

"Hiya Johnny" Jean replies

"Have you had a good day love"

"They never seem to be a good day anymore mum, what about the latest, the judges have now been told not to send burglars to prison if they are on drugs, what they are saying then! Is if you rob peoples homes and you are on drugs you wont be put in the clink, what a shambles, what a state of affairs, sounding very depressed, when Danny walks through from the kitchen with a cup of tea for Jean

"Here you are Mrs Longhurst" putting the cup down on Jeans little table near her wheelchair

"I better get off now Mrs Longhurst" Danny says, Jean then says

"Come here Daniel here's a fiver get yourself some things with it you know John, Daniel is a good boy and I have enjoyed my outing to the shops looking around" when Danny says

"I don't want all that Mrs Longhurst I've enjoyed taking you to the shops"

"Daniel I want you to take it" Johnny then says

"You better take it Danny or she'll get annoyed" Johnny smiling when he says that

"Alright Mrs Longhurst but I don't want anymore when I take you out, I don't take you out for money"

"Alright Daniel, here you are please take it" Danny leans over and Jean kisses him on his cheek, Danny says

"Thank you Mrs Longhurst" and when going out he shouts

"See you Johnny" Johnny replies

"Yea ok Danny bye"

"See you the day after tomorrow Mrs Longhurst is that alright"

"Of course it is Daniel and thank you"

"Bye then"

"Goodbye Daniel" he then leaves.

Fury

Then at the hospital Brenda Jackson sat in the waiting area when Penny James and Paul arrive James runs up to his mother and puts his arms around her and asks

"Where's dad mum is he alright now, I want him to be alright now mum" crying at the same time

"Look dry your eyes James you don't want to show your dad that your crying do you" James still crying says

"No but I want my dad to get better and want him home,

"Look I'll take you through to see him, now be a big boy" James says

"I will mum"

"Good boy come on Penny and you Paul as well" they were all following Brenda towards Jimmy's room on entering, there is a doctor and nurse at his bedside with him, Brenda says

"Is it alright to come in my children are with me now" the doctor says

"Yes of course Mrs Jackson I'm glad your all here, you go to your husband and your father" the doctor says

"If you need us we are only next door" when the doctor and nurse leave, Brenda goes to Jimmy and holds his hand and Penny and James along with Paul goes to the other side of the bed Jimmy opens his eyes then partly open he sees Brenda with a little smile Penny and James holds his other hand Jimmy turns to his children very slowly then with one of his hands he points to himself then touches his heart and then points to Penny and James and Brenda then says

"Your dads telling you he loves you both" Penny then breaks down and says

"Or dad we love you" and James then says

"I do dad I want you to come home why doesn't dad talk mum"

"Your dad has had a stroke so he can't speak at the moment" Brenda looking at Jimmy with tears coming in her eyes, looking at Brenda doing the same signs as he did with Penny and James with tears running down his face with Brenda Penny and James holding his hands he kind of slumps and very still Brenda realises things aren't just right and shouts

"Nurse nurse someone come please" the doctor comes in really quickly with the nurse and says

"We'll see to things could you please stand out side Mrs Jackson with your family we'll be back with you as soon as possible we'll just see what problem we have", outside Penny says and crying

"Mum dads not going to die is he" with James crying sobbing immensely Brenda with tears running down her cheek saying

"No the doctor and nurse are inside with your dad doing there job lets just wait" and at this moment the doctor comes out and looks at Brenda and says

"I'm sorry Mrs Jackson" Brenda says

"Oh god no" and hugs Penny and James with Paul holding them also all extremely distressed the nurse comes and says

"Would you like to come into the room and I will have a cup of tea sent to you, just stay as long as you like"

"Thank you" Brenda replies.

At the police station Pc Kenny Johnson walking through near the desk

"Hiya sarg" to Sergeant Peter Smith

"Hello Kenny lad"

"Eh sarg I've just been reading a piece in the paper about new government plans, could see violent criminals escaping jail by paying a five hundred pound fine people then who are guilty of GBH or possessing heroin and any other serious crime to skip court and not get a jail term by paying a fine a conditional cautioning system could let those carrying a knife affray and criminal damage get off with the fine I think the government has a lot to answer for and now burglars cant be sent to prison if they are on drugs at this moment Inspector Hardy walks up

"Yes Kenny I've just read about what you've just been telling Peter what good people have to look forward to, there is even talk about young nutters been given a wage so they will behave themselves what about the good kids after all, there is more of them, what will they think, hey its better to be bad and we'll get a wage that's what a lot will think" at this time Pc George and Pc Walker arrive

"Hiya sarg"

"Sir" to the Inspector! then turn to Kenny,

"I don't know if you know Kenny we've just come back from the hospital after taking a statement from a guy who was taken in after a mugging and we saw the Jackson family deeply upset, the wife and there kids had found out that Mr Jackson had died I thought I'd tell you because I remember you going to see them about the trouble they was having and how sorry you felt for them" Kenny says

"Yea I did even more so now you've told me that I'll try to go and see them tomorrow" Inspector Hardy then says

"Go see them Kenny"

"Thank you sir" Kenny replies.

The following day Danny walking down the road towards the corner where all his mates hang out, Harry sees Danny and shouts

"Hiya Danny, Joe just heared that bloke who lives near me died last night in hospital, the one where Shaun and his mates smashed all their windows, you Joe and Gerry was down there when someone threw a stone or something at a bus and shattered a window who was that"

"There was a gang of young kids messing about going down there, was that Shaun and his little dicks" Danny says

"Yes but we was well behind them so from a distance ! it was hard to say who threw the stone, it could have been any one of them you'll have to ask them Danny"

"Do you think they'll tell the truth the lying little bastards" Danny replies, at the time Diane walks up

"Hiya Danny" Danny turns and answers

"Hiya Diane what you doing"

"Walking round to see if I could see you" Danny then says

"Well you see me what do you want" Diane says

"I thought we was going out together, you just don't see me no more"

"I've been busy" Danny says

"With one thing and another, I'll see you tonight, you know the saying, get them off later" Diane then turns and says

"You discuss me Danny Laine go to hell"

"Now Diane" Danny shouts

"I'll see you later, you know I fancy you, you silly cow" Diane just doesn't answer and goes, Danny just laughs Harry says

"I think she's chucked you in Danny"
"So what! I can get anybody its not just her that fancies me".

Down the road at the Jackson's where there is a council workman putting in some new windows and inside Penny James Paul and Brenda just doing a sandwich and a drink when a knock on the door, Paul goes to the door and opens it, Paul shouts
"There's a policeman at the door Brenda" Brenda comes through and sees Pc Kenny Johnson stood there
"Come in will you constable what would you like to see us about, you know I lost my husband last night at the hospital"
"Yes I've heard Mrs Jackson, that's why I've come to see you to give you my condolences to you and your family"
"That's nice of you constable would you like to sit down and have a cup of tea your welcome to"
"Yes thank you Mrs
Jackson, call me Kenny if you like, its better than to keep saying constable"
"Ok Kenny" Brenda says, she goes and brings the tea through with some sandwiches
"Help yourself Kenny to sugar and milk and if you would like a sandwich your welcome to that as well" Brenda sitting down with her drink when Kenny says
"I'm sorry that Mr Jackson was a very poorly man and to endure the kind of things that has happened since you have moved here"
"Did he have an heart attack or was it just all the complications he had" Brenda looks at Kenny with glaring eyes and says
"It wasn't any complications that killed my Jimmy it was stress that killed him, the stress that these little bastards round here did to him, the worry the torment and terror of what they was going to do next that's what killed him"
she then starts crying in which Penny and James start crying also, and goes to there mother, a knock on the door, Paul goes, its one of the workman stood there he says
"Just to let you know where finished now, and hope everything's going to be alright" Paul says

Fury

"Thank you" and as the workmen are going through the gate he sees young Shaun with some of his mates Paul starts running towards them when they see him, Shaun shouts

"Run he's coming for us" Paul running he shouts

"I'll get you, you piece of shit" Harry Joe and Danny looking down, Danny says

"Who's that kid running after them" Harry answered and says

"Its that lasses boyfriend who lives there"

"He seems to know that it was Shaun that's been smashing his birds house windows"

"Yes" Harry answers

"He's tried before to catch them" Danny then says

"There's a cop car at the house, wonder if they know who it is, Shaun and his little gang of kids" Harry says

"I don't know but the old bloke who lives there he's dead, it's all over down the street even my old man asked me if I know who it is, I couldn't very well say yea could I, otherwise it will revert back to us after all you told Joe to get his band of kids to smash them up" Danny said

"What are you talking about you silly bastard, its nothing to do with me and if anybody says different they'll regret it so don't talk like a dick"

"Yea alright Danny" Harry answers

"Anyway I want you to find out who threw a stone at my dads bus, my dad could have been hurt" ok!

ok" Harry says.

And back down at the Jackson's Paul comes back in, Brenda says "Did you catch him Paul"

"No I didn't but I will sooner or later that's for sure" Paul answers Kenny says

"Look I'm going now Mrs Jackson, if there's anything I can help you with about getting the people responsible for what they have done just contact me at the station"

"Thank you Kenny it was very good of you to come anyway"

"No problem Mrs Jackson and thank you for the cuppa"

"That's alright" Brenda replies

"Well goodbye and don't forget what I have said"
"Goodbye Kenny" Kenny Johnson then leaves.

At the time Harry and Danny walking towards the usual corner where all the baseball cappers and hoodies are, Joe shouts
"Hiya Danny look at Steve he's had tattoos on both arms" Steve then says
"Look Danny barbed wire tattoos good eh"
"Do you think so, it makes you look hard at least" Danny replies, Steve then says
"I am hard I can take a punch" Danny then says
"Yea you can take punches then you start crying" Danny and some of the lads start laughing, Danny then says to Joe
"Joe I want you to find out if it was one of those little mates of yours who threw a stone at my dads bus, and when you do I want to know straight away"
"Ok Danny" Joe replies
"I'm going now to see Diane, see you sometime tomorrow" Danny says
"See you all"
"See you Danny" the lads and lasses say, Joe says
"Ok what shall we do, lets go wreck some fuckers night, come on" and then they leave about fifteen girls and lads.

Walking down the road they run into Shaun and his little kids, Shaun says
"Hiya Joe where you going" Joe replies
"Around where are you all going" Shaun says
"Where going down to the pensioners bungalows for a bit of fun"
"Yea ok then we'll all come with you, so Joe with the usual lot with Shaun and his little mates walking down to the Laurel Parks Estate where there are mostly pensioners bungalows with open grass fronts they arrive and start chanting, and running along the bungalows banging on the doors and windows completely terrorising the old people, mostly not in the best of health, not dare to go out and complain to the kids knowing it will only make more problems for themselves,

Shaun says1

"Get a dustbin and we'll get on the roof come on" and then they go to the end bungalow down the path, they go into a shed and bring out a ladder, six of them climb up the ladder to get onto the roof, at this time Joe and the older kids take off, on the roof, they start running up and down and banging! some of the pensioners come out, one of the men from the other end bungalow Mr Williams, Bert shouted

"What do you think you are doing up there trying to kill yourselves" Shaun shouted down

"Fuck off you old cunt" Bert then shouted

"I'll old cunt you if I get my hands on you"

"You can't hit me I'm underage" Shaun says, Bert shouts to his wife

"Phone the police Pauline and tell them what's happening here" Shaun then shouts

"Send for the police they can't do fuck all to me either" the other kids on the ground run off when Mrs Williams goes into the bungalow to phone the police, the other kids on the roof says

"Come on Shaun lets go before the cops come" Mr Williams shouts too the other end of the bungalow to the people there "Take that ladder down so the kids can't get down" at this time the kids are getting down from the roof with the old people not dare do anything, Shaun gets down and kicks an old lady who is near. He then picks up a stone and says "Anybody tries to get me and I'll hit them with this stone my names Shaun Taylor and I'm here to stay, then lets fly with the stone at Mr Williams and misses then runs away. Mr Williams then go's in his bungalow and say's to his wife Pauline have you phoned the police, she say's yes they say they will send someone as soon as they can, Mr Williams then say's what help we get is zero, I'll go to the council again tomorrow to see what kind of protection we are likely to get, I've asked many times for them to put up c.c.tv cameras up but nothing, see what they say tomorrow.

Later on the same evening Joe, Harry, Gerry and the rest of the huddies drinking Cider at the old building, when Steve Bean walking in with Pete Lawson and his girlfriend Jackie! Steve says "What 'ya doing! is anything happening"

Joe says

"Not yet have you seen Danny?" asked Joe.

Pete replying

"No why?"

"Oh nothing except I think Diane's chucked him up she thinks he thinks more of Mrs Longhurst than he does of her"

Pete then says

"I think you should mind your own business Joe and don't even mention that again Danny will sort things out like he always does" then Steve Bean buts in.

"Aren't you allowed to say anything"

Pete answers

"Yes but not about things that are private so shut your fucking mouth up before it gets you into trouble"

"Alright" Steve says

"You've no need to get nasty"

Joe says

"Here Pete have a can"

"Yea" Pete says, then Joe says "Right lads later on we'll go down to that fucking posh road and do a bit of damage they can afford it the rich bastards. Jackie then says

"Don't you think the people down there have worked hard for there money and deserve what they have? I don't think you will have anything like they have Joe you haven't got the brains"

"Tell her Pete nobody will get away with what she has just said to me" Pete then says

"What can I say Joe! come on Jackie lets go" Pete and Jackie then walk away arms around each other.

"Even Pete one of my best mates thinks I'm a dick head but I'll show everybody" says Joe

"One day people will shit themselves when they see me"

At the police station the desk sergeant talking to Pc Stan Smith and Pc Dick Charmer

Fury

"Note for you lads! will you go down to see a Mr Williams and some of the residents down Spinny Close on the Laurel Parks Estate at the Pensioners bungalows they've had some trouble with young kids on there roof kicking an old lady and throwing A stone at the gentleman besides running a riot at other bungalows you'll be seeing Mr Williams, both officers say

"Ok Sarg, we'll get statements and bring them in"

"Right o lads, see you later" answers the Sergeant.

But at the same time Mr Williams is on his way to see someone at the council office's, on arriving going to the desk a young lady say's yes sir can I help you, Mr Williams say's can I speak to someone in authority to see if we can get some real help about the young kids that's causing havoc in our area, when a lady a Mrs Clayton came through to the desk, yes sir what problem have you, a big problem that nobody seems to want to help, Bert then asks do you mind if I ask who I am speaking to, Mrs Clayton answers, I am the assistance housing manager, right then, Mr Williams says I would like to know when and so would a lot more people what your intentions are of helping us to live a life in peace on our estate without these hooligans terrorising all of us, a lot of the people living there are mostly in there 80's and worked all there lives both myself and my wife have heart conditions other people with different problems, some are widows and widowers who are very frightened to me that is very unfair that people should live there last years in fear, why cant or should I say! Won't you do anything about this problem, why not have cctv cameras put up, why not have the police patrol more regular or even let some of the police sit in some of the bungalows they will then know what we have to live with, it gets worse at the weekends, they vandalise what ever they feel like doing! This has been going on for along time now and we don't seem to get any help to stamp this out or protection! Mrs Clayton answers by saying! We are aware of this issue on the estate, and we are working together with the police to find a resolution to the problem! Mr Williams answers by saying you are aware of what is happening, then why the hell has nothing been done, this has been happening for about 2 months now, you admit you know and aware of the problem the suffering of the people on the estate you don't seem to care, neither you or the police care, Mrs Clayton then says! Mr Williams we do care, we will be doing everything in our power to sort this problem out it just takes a little time! Mr Williams answers! That's all it takes for these young hooligans to do some real damage to innocent vulnerable people wont it! Walking out Mr Williams says thanks for nothing if I happen to miss a weeks rent I'm sure I will get a quick response with a letter telling me to pay or else wont I.

At the same time Danny trying to sweet talk Diane at her house gate

"Come on Diane, let me in your mum and dads out for at least an hour, if I've done anything wrong which I haven't lets go in a make up you know we both like it" Diane answers by saying

"Danny you can fuck off you wont treat me like shit again, you only want one thing from me which you wont get so go I don't need you" Danny then in a rage says

"Right you cow, I can get anyone you'll see, then you'll come begging" Diane says

"I don't think so, use somebody else"

"Yea I will you can go ballocks now" and then leaves, Diane then looking! then turns away crying and goes into the house.

Joe and his merry men walking down the road near the shops, Joe says, lets go get some boose we'll ask this old bloke to get us six cans of beer from the shop the old man near the shops when Joe says

"Excuse me Mr can you get me six cans of beer for me dad he can't get out he's broke his leg" the gent says

"No I'm not getting into trouble by getting you beer"

"It's not for me it's for me dad" Joe says

"I'm sorry I wont" answers the old gentleman

"Right you silly old bastard I'll get you" says Joe, Harry then says

"Come on Joe we've had plenty"

"Yea but I'll get that old cunt, hang around a bit I want to see where he lives" Gerry says

"Catch us up then Joe" as Joe is waiting he sees Jason

"Hiya Jase where you going"

"Nowhere" replies Jason

"What you doing round here Joe"

Fury

"Waiting for this old fart to come out the shop I want to know where he lives" Jason asks

"Why" Joe says

"All I wanted was some cans of beer to get for me dad and he wouldn't he more or less told me to fuck off, hey here he comes Jason don't let him see us" the elderly gent only lives five doors away from the shop, Jason says

"I'll just fill my lighter up then I'll come with you, wherever your going" Joe says

"Give us that petrol can Jason, and I'll squirt it all over him I've got a box of matches I'll let him get warm" Jason says

"You know where he lives! see to it on your own! come on I'm off" Jason walks away then Joe follows catching the rest of the gang up

"Hiya Jason" Harry says

"Hiya lads" Jason replies

"Where you going"

"Just for a walk around you coming Jason" Steve asks

"Yea might as well nothing else to do" Jason says, walking towards Belvedere Avenue, Joe says

"Look at all these big fucking houses with there posh fucking walls and gates and fences, we'll let them know we've been" Joe starts booting a wooden fence and smashes some wood off, he takes that and starts hitting other parts of the fence, some of the other kids join in Jason Steve and Harry starts pushing at the wall until about three layers of bricks start coming off they then start pushing at a brick post until the top piece comes away Joe says

"Come and pick some of these bricks up and throw them into the wooden fencing" and they did making a compete mess running up the road with bricks throwing them at wooden fences and smashing it up! Gerry says

"Ok lets go now we can always come back before anyone see's us, give us something to do another time" so they all ran off laughing, Steve says

"What good jobs we've done eh Joe, what do you think Jason"

"Good laugh" Jason replies.

Don Fleming

The next day at the police station at the desk when Inspector Hardy walks through the Sergeant says

"Good morning Sir"

"Good morning?" when Pc Smith and Pc Dick Charmer come in

"Send them through to my office will you"

"Sir before you go in we've got a few complaints from residents down Belvedere Avenue a lot of the houses fencing and walls was destroyed" the Inspector said

"Did anyone see anything, any names we can go on"

"No Sir just send someone to see them at the houses which were damaged" answers Inspector Hardy

"Will do Sir" replies the Sergeant.

Down at Mrs Longhurst's expecting Danny! Jean sitting in her chair having a drink of tea dressed for the weather conditions when a knock on the door and enters Danny

"Hiya Mrs Longhurst, I said I would be here"

"You did Daniel it's a very hot Sunny morning and the weather man said it will get hotter about ninety degrees so I am taking a bottle of water with me in a cool bag"

"Alright Mrs Longhurst whatever"

"Well I'm ready Daniel"

"Ok Mrs Longhurst lets go" Danny pushed Jean in her chair, up to and outside the door

"Here Daniel the keys to lock the door" Danny locks up and gives Jean her keys back

"Right Mrs Longhurst where do you want to go"

"I'd like you to take me to the shops" said Jean, so off they go up the road towards the shops.

Down at the corner where the usual louts hang around Steve acting big and good in front of the girls that's there, showing his tattoos off he then says

"I'm going to get the skull and crossbones tattoo next" when up the road walking Mrs Parker and her son, the lad with learning disabilities Steve says

Fury

"Eh look who's coming up, that mongee" as Mrs Parker is nearing! Steve shouts

"Eh mongee come here so I can smack you up" Mrs Parker says

"You wont touch him" at this time Billy Ford is walking up from the opposite direction and says

"That's right you wont touch him I see your still playing the high and mighty, why don't you look for someone who will accommodate you eh" nobody says anything Mrs Parker says

"Thank you Mister"

"Don't mention it love" Billy answers

"They think that they are big, but on there own their different aren't you ginger bollocks" then Billy looks at Joe

"I haven't said anything Billy" Joe says, Billy doesn't answer just walks on, at this time Shaun comes up with a couple of his mates shouts

"Hiya Joe"

"Hiya Shaun where you going" asks Joe

"Nowhere just walking around, we might go back to the pensioners bungalow again they think they can tell us what to do the silly old farts! at this time Paul! Penny Jackson's boyfriend and some of his friends with him says at the time he grabs Shaun by the neck

"Got you, you little arsehole I was told you hung about up here now your going to the police station with us"

"I haven't done anything" Shaun says

"But you have you little piece of shit, you've done your best to kill my girlfriends father by smashing all there windows and put him in hospital where he died with your help so your coming now" Shaun shouts

"Joe Steve Harry help me" Paul says looking at the rest of them

"Don't even think about it" Paul then drags Shaun away with his friends heading to the police station.

Steve says

"What are we going to do now" Harry says

"I know what I'm going to do, let Danny know it was Shaun who threw the stone at his old mans bus, that idiot Shaun is in deep shit now"

At the station Paul taking Shaun into the police station! at the desk Shaun trying to get away but Paul holding and twisting his arm Shaun squeeling and crying, the Sergeant says

"Hey what are you doing to that lad" Paul says

"Ask him why he's here and if he doesn't tell you the truth I'll tell you"

the Sergeant asks

"Why have you been brought in boy" Shaun says

"I haven't done anything"

"In that case contact Mrs Jackson at two nine three" replies Paul

"Phone number six four six nine five one it would also help if you contact Pc Kenny Johnson who has been dealing with the case of Mrs Jackson's windows been put through lots of times, by this thing and his mates" at this time Pc Turner and Pc Anderson coming through to go out of the station when Pc Bill Turner was looking at the lad Shaun and said

"What's he in for Sarg, walking on roofs"

"No! why did you ask that" Pc Turner replies by saying

"Because he fits a description that Mr Williams gave us" the Sergeant then turns to Shaun and says

"Is it you that's been playing havock at the pensioners bungalows" Shaun replies by saying

"I don't know what he's talking about"

"Well in that case we'll contact Mr Williams to come up here"

"What are you doing now Bill" asks the Sergeant

"Just going out Sir"

"Right then I'll phone Mr Williams and Mrs Jackson and if they're available pick them up and bring them here if you will"

"On my way Sarg" answers Pc Turner

"Now then lad we'll soon know if you're telling the truth".

Up at the shops Danny with Jean, and Jean looking round Willy's Store Danny pushing her in the wheelchair Jean with a basket on her knee picking up things that she wants to buy

"Look Daniel" Jean says looking at some wrist watches

"Aren't they nice for the price there only six ninety nine would you like one Daniel" Danny says

"No you're alright Mrs Longhurst"

"Go on you haven't got a watch have you"

"No but it's alright" Danny says

"Come on let me buy you one you deserve it if it wasn't for you I wouldn't be going out shopping would I, so come on have a look and pick one out" Danny looks at the watches and picks one

"I like this one Mrs Longhurst"

"Right Daniel if that's the one you like I'd like to buy it for you" Jean says, they walk to the payout desk to pay for it and the other items after that they leave.

At the police station the Sergeant moves the boys out of sight and leaves young Shaun sat on a chair, in visible sight of the entrance door to the station Pc Turner enters with Mr Williams and Mrs Jackson and straight away Mr Williams sees Shaun sat down and says

"I see you've got that little lout who was on the roofs of the bungalows and threw a stone at me"

"Are you saying that, that is the lad who was there and did what you say" asks the Sergeant

"That is definitely the scum that was the main piece of shit that was there with his little pals" answers Mr Williams, Mrs Jackson then says

"I saw him with his mates throwing stones and smashing our windows, he was with his pals, they was the main cause of my husbands death" the Sergeant then says

"Right lad you are under arrest and your parents will be informed when you give us your full name and address"

"Bill" says the Sergeant!

"Take the lad and get a full statement on both accounts of the problem he is in here for, get a phone number from him and let me have it"

"Ok Sarg" answers Pc Turner, at the time Paul and his mates come from another direction Mrs Jackson looks and says!

"What are you doing here Paul" Paul replies by saying

"I saw the piece of dirt and we brought him to the station hopefully he'll get his just reward"

"I hope" answers Mrs Jackson
"I do hope so".

At this time Danny just getting back to Mrs Longhurst Danny pushing Jean into the house Jean says!
"Can you put the shopping in the kitchen Daniel our John will see to things when he comes home"
"Ok Mrs Longhurst" Danny replies after taking Jeans shopping through Danny says
"Anything else Mrs Longhurst"
"No thank you Daniel you're a good boy put your watch on you might as well wear it now it will look good on you"
"Thank you Mrs Longhurst for the watch I can take you out again the day after tomorrow if you want"
"That would be lovely Daniel"
"Anyway I'll go now Mrs Longhurst"
"Thank you again Daniel" Jean says
"Come here love let me give you a kiss" Danny leans over and kisses Jean on her lips
"Daniel" says Jean
"You shouldn't kiss me on the lips"
"I know I'm sorry Mrs Longhurst"
"Oh alright Daniel" Danny looking down admiring Jeans busty breasts
"Right I'll go now Mrs Longhurst see you the day after tomorrow if you want"
"That will be fine Daniel"
"What time about ten o clock will that be alright Mrs Longhurst"
"It will be Daniel"
"I'm sorry again Mrs Longhurst"
"Don't worry Daniel see you" Danny then leaves.

Walking home he runs into Joe Steve and Harry, Harry says
"Danny! the kid who threw that stone at your dads bus is that young kid Shaun" Danny says
"The little bastard" Joe then says

Fury

"At the moment he's at the cop shop some kids came and grabbed him and took him by his neck it looked like that kid who knocks around with that lass at the house where the windows had been smashed in down near Harry's" Danny then says

"I'll have him when he gets away with that then"

"What you doing tonight Danny" asks Steve

"With you not going out with Diane now" Danny then answers

"If your trying to be funny beany I'll straighten your fucking eyes for you"

"I didn't mean anything I thought you might want to come with us were going to nick a car and have a ride out do you fancy it"

"No" says Danny

"Try to fucking kill yourself while your at it! anyway I'm going" Danny then turns away to go home Joe shouts

"See you Danny" Danny just replies by saying

"Yea" Joe says

"I think Danny's upset because him and Diane have finished" at this time Jason and a couple of his mates walking up Jason says

"Where you going lads"

"To nick a car, do you want to come" Steve says!

"Why not" answers Jason!

"Nothing else to do" starting to get a little darker the lads take off down the road.

The following day at the youth court Shaun coming out with his mum and dad after receiving a referral order Mr Williams coming out along with Mrs Jackson Mr Williams saying

"Isn't it marvellous what these things get" Mrs Jackson says

"Yes nothing to what hurt they give to people they terrorise, and with the law being on there side they'll continue to do what they want to and continue to get away with it" Mr Williams then says

"You know Mrs Jackson I was reading the paper just the other day and it showed photos from way back in the nineteen twenties there were these very naughty boys in there clothes of that particular age they all got the birch for doing what they had done and now if any of them get into any more trouble they would get the same again but infact they finish being very responsible people afterwards that's the difference of today" Mrs Jackson then answers by saying

"If they did that to these dirt bags today it would be classed as in humain by these so called do gooders, they say you can't fight fire with fire what are you expected to do because the law wont help the good people who just wants to make the best out of life for themselves and there family this asbo crap that was bought out for these bastards wont do anything except let them still do as they like"

"Your right Mrs Jackson! it's been nice to have met you and spoke to you and I wish you all the very best for the future to what you have had to endure" Mr Williams says!

"Thank you" Mrs Jackson replies,

"And all the nice things for you and your family" both saying there goodbye's and going there different ways.

At the police station Pc Bill Turner walking towards inspector Hardy and saying

"That lad Shaun got away with what he's been up to Sir"

"What happened Bill"

"He got a referral order slapped on him two hours a week so he can get help and talked to! what ever that will do"

"I don't know" the Sergeant then comes through

"Sir" to Inspector Hardy

"The car that was reported stolen early this morning had been found burned out at the moment nothing to go on"

"Alright Sergeant If anybody needs me I'll be in my office"

"Yes sir" answers the Sarg, Pc Kenny Johnson comes through

"Morning everybody" Bill says

"Hey Kenny that young kid what did the damage down at the Jackson's got away with it referral order"

"Nothing new that Bill I'm surprised they didn't give him a day out at a fun park".

At Mrs Longhurst's Johnny just ready for leaving for work when a knock on the door and enters Danny

"Hello Mrs Longhurst, hello Johnny"

Fury

"Hello Danny" Johnny says just going, Johnny kisses his mum and says

"I'll be home later tonight mum do you want me to bring you anything home"

"No John I'll get what I need to get while Daniel is taking me to the shops"

"Ok then mum see you later"

"Ok John have a nice day and drink plenty of water its going to be another hot day again today"

"See you mum, bye Danny"

"Yea ok Johnny, right Mrs Longhurst I see your ready" Jean wearing an open neck see through blouse"

"I am Daniel will you please pass me my bottled water"

"I will Mrs Longhurst and I would like to say you look very nice and cool"

"Why thank you Daniel that's nice of you to say! come on then Daniel lets go"

"Ok Mrs Longhurst" Daniel looking and really admiring Jean walking through and locking the door after himself and up the road to the shopping centre.

Down the road at the usual corner are the usual crowd of girls and boys playing football on the causeway kicking it really anywhere going on the road with the cars swerving as the kids run on the road getting the ball back, cars breaking and stopping! with mostly the girls shouting

"Fuck off you idiots" to the drivers in the cars one man who breaks and stops gets out of the car and shouts

"Are you sick of living you lot" they start giving him the two fingered sign then Joe says

"Fuck off or we'll smash your fucking windows" and the cars behind him hooting there horns, the man gets back into his vehicle and drives away the kids start chanting

"Yea fuck off this is our area" and they are chanting to other motorists going by when one of the girls says

"Hey look a fucking funeral parade coming lets give them some shit as they are passing" Joe says

Don Fleming

"Get them eggs out of Jenny's shopping bag and throw them" in which they did four of the girls and two of the boys got one each and threw them at the hurst and the second car with the close family of the deased inside! one person in the second car on his mobile phones to the police to inform them what was happening on the corner the kids still chanting calling names also using the two fingered salute when Steve says

"Hey Joe lets go do something else something better"

"Yea why not the cops will be here soon come on then lets go up town" and they leave, leaving the rest behind.

At the Laine's having lunch Jill and Joe eating and talking

"You know Joe our Danny's very good taking Jean out in the wheelchair when he could be out with his mates" Jill says, Joe answers

"His our Danny still knocking around with that lass of Fred Pearson, Diane I think they call her"

"Yes they do Joe" answers Jill

"I think he is I'm not sure, talking about lads our Shaun will be home at tea time for his summer holidays from collage wont he"

"He'll probably knock around with our Danny a while"

"I don't think so Joe our Shaun don't like our Danny's friends our Shaun thinks they are all idiots" says Jill, Joe answers by saying that

"They've all been polite enough with me".

On there way back to Jeans Danny pushing Jean up the path to the front door, he opens and pushes Jean inside, Jean says

"Will you put the shopping in the kitchen Daniel if you could put the stuff in the cupboard near the table and the meats and eggs in the fridge there's a darling"

"Alright Mrs Longhurst" Danny doing that job comes into the room

"O its hot isn't it Daniel" Danny looking down at her open neck blouse at her Breasts

"Yes it is Mrs Longhurst would you like me to make you a cup of tea"

"Yes I would Daniel, they say tea is more refreshing than anything so yes I will" Jean replies, Danny goes into the kitchen to put the kettle

Fury

on and on walking back through into the room Jean is wiping her neck with a hankiechief Danny looking on then he says

"You're a very lovely looking woman Mrs Longhurst" Jean replies and says

"Thank you Daniel" at this time Danny walking nearer to Jean admiring her breasts he then leans over kisses Jean on the lips

"O Daniel" Jean says

"What was that for"

I know you are older than me Jean and as he leans over again he says

"But I love you" he kisses Jean again on the lips and puts one of his hands on Jeans breasts

"Daniel don't do that he then gives Jean another kiss on the lips, a more passionate one and at the same time opens up her blouse fully he then says

"I've always wanted to do this Jean I love you"

"Daniel, Daniel" Jean pleads

"Don't do that" but Daniel is now very high on having sex, Danny a big stropping lad that he his lifts Jean with a struggle out of her chair onto the floor he then starts raping Jean at this time Jean is saying

"No no please Daniel don't please" she then starts crying and saying

"O please god no" but Danny then starts having sex with her Jean then seems to go into shock, after raping Mrs Longhurst he puts her clothes back on the best way he could and then lifts her back onto the wheelchair he gives her another kiss on the lips and says

"That was brilliant Jean we'll do it again" Jean just sat in shock with tears running down her face but before leaving Danny takes twenty pound from Jean's purse and then leaves.

Jean is crying and shaking her head saying

"Why, o why did this happen why should he do this to me" Jean then picks the phone up and phones the police station at the other end the Sergeant answers the phone

"Hello hello" Jean says

"Is that the police station" the Sergeant says

"Yes can I help you" still crying Jean says

"Can you contact my son John Longhurst please"

"Yes Mrs Longhurst" answers the Sergeant

"Are you alright" Jean replies by saying

"No I need my son to come home as soon as possible you must tell him please tell him"

"Alright Mrs Longhurst I'll contact Johnny now" still crying

"Yes thank you and puts the phone down, at this time Danny has gone home.

Walking through the back door into the kitchen where his mother is making tea

"O hello Danny how have you been today where did you take Mrs Longhurst" Danny replies by saying

"She wanted to go shopping so we went to the shops" saying this a bit sharp

"Hey I'm your mother! be careful with your tone of voice"

"Sorry mum I'm just a little mixed up" Mrs Laine looks up and says

"What do you mean you're a little mixed up"

"Or leave it at that mum"

"Alright you'll tell me when your ready ok" answers Mrs Laine.

Back at Mrs Longhurst's Johnny pulls up out front of the house and runs down the path into the house and sees the state his mother's in Jean still sobbing

"O John I'm pleased your home" Johnny goes to his mother and Jean grabs Johnny's hand she was shaking and crying, tears streaming down her face

"I haven't known what to do" John says

"Mum what's the matter" Jean said shaking says

"John I've been raped by Daniel" John says what

"Danny, how when" Jean says

"When he brought me back home after shopping, I feel dirty"

"Ok mum I'll phone the station and have a warrant taken out on this thing that's done this" John gets through to the station and informs the Sergeant what has happened, the Sergeant then says

Fury

"Ok Johnny I'll get straight onto it give me the persons name and address and I'll send someone out to pick him up" in which Johnny gives the Sergeant, the Sarg calls in Detective Constable Ivor Jones after receiving the warrant to pick Danny up, the Sergeant says

"Take Charlie Paterson with you Ivor I will tell you the person your going to pick up is Susan Laine's brother Daniel Laine for the rape of Mrs Jean Longhurst, yes Ivor Johnny's mother" Ivor then says

"The dirty little bastard Johnny's mother is an invalid she's hardly any use in her body I'll get Charlie and we'll go and get this little shit head ok Sarg"

"Ok Ivor, but stay calm you've a job to do and a responsibility" Ivor leaves to pick up Detective Paterson.

Back at Mrs Longhurst's Johnny getting his mother ready to take her to the hospital so she can be examined

"Come on mum" Johnny says, Jean still sobbing she says

"I feel so embarrassed and dirty John" John says

"Why should you be I'm with you mum"

"I know John, I know"

"Come on mum lets go" they both leave for the hospital.

Down at the Laine's Detective's Jones and Paterson arrive at the front door and ring the doorbell, Joe Laine comes to the door and opens it and says

"Yes" Ivor says

"I am Detective Ivor Jones with my partner Detective Charlie Paterson, does Daniel Laine live here"

"Yes" says Joe the two officers said

"We have a warrant" in which they showed to Mr Laine

"For the arrest of Daniel Laine for the suspected rape of Mrs Jean Longhurst" Joe says

"You must be joking my son runs errands and takes Mrs Longhurst out in her wheelchair to the shops you have got the wrong name and address" when Jill Laine comes to the door

"What's wrong" Joe says

"These two policeman have come to arrest our Danny for the rape of Mrs Longhurst"

"Impossible" Jill answers, Jill shouts for Danny to come to the front door when he doesn't come she goes through to the kitchen where she finds the back door open and Danny had gone out she then goes back to the front door she says

"Joe! Danny's gone out" Ivor says

"Alright Mr and Mrs Laine if we haven't picked Danny up before he comes home please bring him to the station" Joe says

"Alright Detective we will we want this sorted out as well" they then leave and Joe and Jill close the door and go into the room, Joe says to Jill

"This can't be right what the hell's happening"

"I don't know Joe but why did our Danny leave when the police came"

"I don't know lass" answers Joe

"Maybe he didn't know the police had come and just went out you know our Danny always goes out the back way anyway" Joe then says

"Well we'll know what has happened if anything did concerning our Danny when we see him" when the front door opens and in walks Shaun

"Hiya mum and dad" Jill looks and says

"Oh Shaun its nice to see you" Joe also says

"Its good to see you lad" Jill then putting her arms round Shaun.

Later down at the derelict site Danny with Pete Lawson and some of the young kids Danny talking to Pete

"The cops are looking for me Pete"

"What for Danny"

"You don't tell anybody Pete or we'll fall out big time"

"No I wont you know that Danny" at this time Jason walks through with some of his mates

"Hiya Danny" then Danny says to Pete

"I'll tell you later" then shouts back

"Hiya Jason"

"Have you seen Joe" Jason asks

"No I haven't I saw him earlier with some of the lads going towards up town" answers Pete

"Ah well I'll probably see them later do you want a can" asks Jason

Fury

"No answers Danny I'll have to go home see you later Pete see you lads"

"Yea ok Danny" they answer, Danny runs off home.

At the Longhurst's Johnny and Jean having just arrived back from the hospital Jean still very upset and crying Johnny says

"Come on mum let me make you a drink and something to eat"

"No John I don't want anything to eat just a drink"

"Ok mum" answers John when a knock on the door John walks across the room and opens the door there's Detective Ivor Jones there

"Come in Ivor" Johnny says, Ivor walks in looks at Jean

"Hello Mrs Longhurst how are you feeling" Johnny says

"My mother's not to good Ivor" Ivor looking pitiful at Jean and saying

"Sorry Mrs Longhurst" touching her hand, Jean looks up at Ivor with tears in her eyes

"Thank you Ivor, thank you"

"That's alright Mrs Longhurst, can I just see your Johnny for a couple of minutes Mrs Longhurst" Johnny says

"Yea that's ok I'm just making mum a drink come in the kitchen Ivor wont be a minute mum" Mrs Longhurst just sits and says nothing, in the kitchen Ivor says to Johnny

"We've been to the Laine's he had gone out that little toss head but we'll be waiting for him Johnny I've left Charlie Paterson near to the Laine's house he's got to come home sooner or later and as soon as we pick him up we'll let you know Johnny"

"Ok and thanks Ivor"

"That's alright Johnny I'll leave you to see to your mothers drink I'll let myself out see you soon"

"Yea see you Ivor" Ivor walking through the room puts his hand on Jeans shoulder and says

"See you again Mrs Longhurst" Jean says

"Goodbye Ivor" who walks up to the door and lets himself out.

At the Laine's Danny comes in through the back door as he is entering Jill rushes through and says Danny what's been happening at Mrs Longhurst the police have been here with a warrant for your arrest and as Joe walks through a knock on the front door Shaun goes to answer it opens the door and there is both Detective Jones and Paterson, Ivor says

"Daniel Laine" Shaun says

"No but just a moment" and then shouts his dad Joe comes through to see the two Detectives and says

"Yes will you come in" Ivor and Charlie enter the living room where Danny is stood near his mother Ivor says

"Daniel Laine we have a warrant for your arrest in the connection with the rape of Mrs Jean Longhurst anything you may now say can be used in evidence against you we will be taking you to the police station for you to give a written statement about this allegation" Joe says

"What have you to say son"

"I haven't done anything dad" Danny replies! Ivor says!

"We are going to take your son" Joe says

"Can I come with him" Ivor says

"You may do Sir" they then leave leaving Jill with Shaun.

After driving to the station getting out of the car walking up and through the doors of the station through some more doors into a waiting area Ivor says

"If you can sit there with your son Sir and someone will come through to see you shortly alright Sir"

"Yes alright " Joe answers, Joe then turns to Danny and says

"Right what have you done lad" Danny says

"I know they will blame me for everything but its not all my fault" at this time a constable comes through and says

"Daniel Laine come with me please" Joe says

"Can I come" the constable says

"No Sir not at this moment you will be informed Sir".

In Inspector Hardy's office there is the Inspector with Ivor

"Right Ivor you can do the interview with this lad"

"Thank you sir"

"But remember Ivor you are a policeman not an SS officer you know your duty and what your to do and don't make it personal I'll phone Johnny and let him know we've picked Daniel Laine up"

"Alright sir I'll do what you expect of me"

"Good lad" Inspector Hardy replies.

Ivor goes through to the office were Danny is, Danny sat down in front of a desk just looking at Ivor, Ivor sits at the other side and says

"Now then Daniel I'd like you to give a statement of events at Mrs Jean Longhurst's home we know you took Mrs Longhurst to the shops etc and we want a statement from when you took her into her home from going in and coming out alright do you understand what I'm talking about answer yes or no" Daniel answers

"Yes" Officer Jones then says

"From what you say is being recorded between the both of us do you understand that" Danny answers again

"Yes" Ivor then says

"In your own words Daniel from getting back into Mrs Longhurst's house what happened, when your ready Daniel"

Daniel then says

"Right first it looks like I'm being blamed for raping Mrs Longhurst well I didn't rape her but yes I did have sex with her she encouraged me when I got back I was going to make a cup of tea for her and when I came back into the room she asked me to come to her so I did then she kissed me on the lips she opened her blouse and put my hand on one of her tits she then started to feel me below and then got hold of my dick and started messing about with it she then asked me to go further and put my hand down her private place I was then starting to get high and just wanted to have her so I did I put her things back on like she asked me to and then she gave me another kiss and gave me twenty pounds and that's what happened I wouldn't of done anything but she wanted me to and now I feel guilty of what happened but it wasn't all my fault"

"Right Daniel" Ivor says

wright that up and sign it alright" Danny says

"Yes I will".

Back at the Laine's Susan comes home and says

"A person at work told me our Danny's been charged with the rape of Mrs Longhurst that can't be right can it" Jill says

"No"

"I don't know what happened but I can't see our Danny doing anything wrong he runs all over for Jean" Shaun then says

"You don't know mother what our Danny is capable of" Jill then shouts at Shaun

"What are you saying your supposed to be on your brothers side"

"Mother" answers Shaun

"I can't really see Mrs Longhurst raping our Danny can you?"

"Well something's happened" Jill replied

"And I can't see our Danny doing wrong"

"What are you saying mum that it must be Mrs Longhurst's fault? And you're her friend!"

"Oh shut up Shaun"

And at Mrs Longhurst with Johnny with her also detective Jones! Ivor saying

"Johnny if your mum is too upset and not well enough to make a statement I can come back tomorrow"

Johnny says

"That might be best Ivor"

"Alright Johnny" then Ivor touching Jeans hand saying

"I'll see ya' tomorrow Mrs Longhurst"

Jean crying and in a state of shock didn't answer.

Back at the station Danny has given a statement of events when inspector Hardy goes to see Joe to tell him that Danny will have to stay there in the cells until the following day to be taken to court to see what the magistrate will have done Joe says

"Can't he come home with me on bail?" Inspector Hardy says

"I'm afraid not sir it's a serious offence your son has been arrested and charged! with only the magistrates can decide on bail otherwise he will have to stay here sorry sir but they are the rules we have to go by"

Joe then leaves to go home.

The following day down at the derelict buildings there's the usual gang with Joe, Steve, Harry, Gerry, Jason and some of his mates , Pete Lawson, Petes girlfriend Jackie and the rest of the baseball caps and hoodies Harry says

Fury

"Danny's been arrested for the rape on Mrs Longhurst I called round this morning and his brother told me" Jason says

"He must have been desperate" Joe then says

"Mind you she gives him money maybe she pays him for it" Pete then says

"If I was you I'd keep my thoughts to myself you know what Danny's like if you talk about him" Then Jackie says

"What will poor old Diane think when she finds out" Pete says

"Not much she can do" Harry says

"He's still in the nick until he goes in front of a judge" Steve then says

"They'll have to let him out because he's only young" Pete says

"Maybe and maybe not who knows".

Back at Mrs Longhurst's Johnny says to Jean

"Mum I'm going to have to phone and let our Frankie know what's happened" Jean says!

"No not yet John he may do something what he shouldn't do and be very upset remember he's on the rigs John! and he could have an accident by worry"

"I understand what you are saying mum but he will have to know" Johnny replies

"Not yet John"

"Ok mum" Johnny answers

"Will you be alright to make a statement for Ivor mum when he comes, Jean says

"Not really but I know I will have to live through it again what happened" she then starts crying

"Come on mum" Johnny puts his arms around his mother to comfort her when a knock on the door and enters Pauline, she walks over to Jean who is still crying and gives her a cuddle Jean says

"Thank you Pauline I'll be alright in a minute"

"Jean let me make you and Johnny a drink" when at this time another knock on the door and Johnny goes to answer and opens the door, it's Shaun Laine stood there

"Can I come in Johnny and see your mum" Johnny says

"Are you sure you want to Shaun" Shaun says

"Yes I do"

"Then come in" Johnny answers! Shaun looks at Jean and says

"I'm very sorry for you Mrs Longhurst our Danny has done a bad thing to you and I believe he did what he was arrested for I know our Danny a lot more than my mum and dad know him, I know what he is really like he uses people for his own self, my sister knows what he's like but she wont admit it I've just come to say I'm very sorry for what has happened" Jean says

"Thank you Shaun thank you for coming to see and tell me! thank you Shaun"

"I'll go now Mrs Longhurst I just had to come and see you" Johnny says

"Thanks Shaun it's good of you to come" Johnny going to the door and letting Shaun out as Shaun is walking up the path passing on the other side of the road there is Joe Downs and the rest of the gang Joe looks across and see's Shaun coming out of the gate Joe looks across and says

"Hey Shaun" Shaun looks across when Joe shouts

"You just been in to see if you can dip your wick then" and starts laughing Shaun says

"Come here Downsie and let me smack your silly looking face" Joe never said anything else and went! then walking up the road with the rest of his merry men.

Joe says

"Aye Jason should we go up to that idiot with the second hand shop! him who we smashed up"

"Yea why not" Jason answered so off they went putting their hoods up over their baseball caps.

Back at the police station Ivor who has been to see Mrs Longhurst for a statement from her walking through to see inspector Hardy he runs into Chief inspector McClure

"Hello Ivor have you got a statement from Johnny's mother?"

"Yes sir I was just going through to see the inspector"

"I was going through myself"

Fury

So they both walked through into inspector Hardy's office who is sat behind his desk. Chief McClure says

"Don't get up George" to the inspector

"I was just popping to see you and then I ran into Ivor who has the statement from Johnny's mother about the incident and talking about the incident that young lad Daniel Laine has been to court and the magistrate has referred it to crown court with it being so serious the lads solicitor has asked for bail with him being a young lad until a date set for a trial the prosecution solicitor agreed but only with an electronic tag and to come to the station daily at 4:30 pm and until the trial Johnny will be on compassionate leave to stay with his mum to do what he has to do for her also Susan Laine will be missing from work after she spoke to me by phone she also feels very upset about what has happened and she wouldn't be able to cope with her work. Under the circumstances so there we are anyway Ivor how is Johnny and Mrs Longhurst coping with things"

"Johnny's mother is very distressed she looks very tired being she is not sleeping and she is crying nearly all of the time, I think sir! Johnny has a hard job to do"

Down at the second hand shop all of the gang there when Jason says

"Why don't we put a brick through his window?" Joe then says

"Who owns that land rover in front of his shop?"

Jason says

"He does"

"And who owns that wheelie-bin?" Jason says

"I don't know may be his why?"

then Steve says

"I know what your thinking Joe lets do it" they go across the road empty the wheelie bin on the pathway then they lift the bin up and smash it through the front window of the truck Steve then runs into the shop and says

"Hey Mr you've just had a wheelie bin rammed into the front window of your truck outside" then turned away and ran off laughing Steve catches the rest up, they're all laughing about what they have done Joe says

"When he's got it repaired we'll do it again" they all just take off up the road.

At the rig were Frankie works His Foreman Peter Taylor goes to see Frankie
Walking up to him Peter says
"Frankie there has been a phone call from your brother Johnny for you to contact him as soon as possible" Frankie says
"Did he say what for"
"No" answers Peter
"Come up to the office and contact him from there", they reach the office and Frankie then uses the phone and contacts his home Johnny answers and Frankie says
"What's the matter Johnny" Johnny then explains everything to Frankie, Frankie then answers
"The fucking little bastard" Johnny says
"Everything has been taken care of by the police he'll be going to crown court when a date is fixed"
"And he has been charged with the rape then Johnny" answers Frankie
"What will happen to the scumbag I'll tell you Johnny Fuck all, probably a holiday in Hawaii" Johnny says
"I can understand what your saying Frankie I'm also upset for what has happened Frankie but I'm off work looking after mother until the time comes that she'll be alright so I'll keep you in touch she's in safe hands, Pauline's still coming in" Frankie says
"I'll come home to help"
"No everything's alright at the moment Frankie" Johnny says
"I'll keep you up to date with what's happening everyday so you'll know alright Frankie"
"Ok Johnny" answers Frankie
"But even so I'll be coming home at the weekend no matter what"
"Alright then Frankie can you ring me tomorrow at about six o clock then I can tell you what kind of day mother has had" Frankie says
"Ok I'll ring you! then tell mum I love her"
"Alright Frankie" they then say there goodbyes.

Fury

Later on in the evening the usual gang is starting to go there own ways probably to do there own thing. Joe and Jason walking down the road at this time the Stones brothers just passing them going in the same direction when Ronnie said

"Hey Jim isn't that the two lads we want who we just passed?" Jim says

"Yea pull up round the corner get the motor bike helmets on and get the wooden batons just for the job" Ronnie says!

"Where in luck Jim nobody about waiting just round the corner as Joe and Jason get there" Ronnie and Jim jump out Ronnie belts Joe and Jim belts Jason they both dropped to the ground and as the stone boys look round to see if there is anybody around they both boot the two lads Joe says

"Don't hit us where only 14 years old where only school boys" Ronnie picks Joe up at the time and says

"But you beat old ladies up don't you and rob them" Joe says

"No not us" Ronnie then says

"Don't fucking lie to me bastard" at the same time Jason says

"I haven't done anything why did you hit me?" Jim then kicks Jason in the face

"You're a lying little bastard as well aren't you? Are you trying to tell me you didn't rob an old lady and set fire to her home? If you don't tell me the truth you keep your mouth shut or I'll club it closed" Ronnie gets Joe down on the floor and says

"Which knee do you want kneecapping" Joe starts crying and says

"Please don't I promise I won't do anything wrong again" at this moment Ronnie bats Joes knee with the wooden baton three times, Joe starts screaming with pain Ronnie then says

"That's so you don't forget what you just promised because if you don't we'll be back to do the other one" that's when Jim gives Jason the same.

"Please, please" Jason screams out

"I've had enough" Jim then kicks Jason in the mouth and says

"No you haven't you can still speak" Ronnie and Jim then goes leaving the two lads in a lot of pain screaming and crying on the ground. A police car coming up the road the two policemen Pc George Taylor and Pc Roger Dent

"Hey George look there on the ground our friend Downsey" the police car pulls up and both of the officers get out and goes up to both lads on the ground both holding there knee

"You better ring through for an ambulance George it looks like they have been well and truly beaten up"

"Ok Roger will do"

"Well Downsie who did it" Joe says

"Two rotten bastards with bike helmets on! it could have been any bastard" Joe crying and holding his knee along with Jason, Pc Dent says

"It must have been somebody you've done something to! do you think" Jason says

"we have done nothing to nobody they just hit us the fucking cowards" George comes back

"Ambulance on it's way Roger I've informed the station as well" then coming up the road with a siren on and flashing blue lights an ambulance pulls up and two medics get out, one medic says

"We will have to check them to see what injuries they have" after both medics examine the lads one medic says to the officers

"They've both got busted kneecaps we'll get them both on stretchers and rush them to hospital" with the police officers assistants they get both lads in the ambulance and set off siren and flashing lights, George says to Roger

"It had to happen in time" Roger then says

"Well one thing George they may be able to hide but they wont be able to run now,

"Come on lets go Roger" the officers get into the car and leave.

The day after at the Longhurst's Johnny says

"Mum you haven't eaten any of your breakfast" Jean says

"I don't feel like anything John I only need a drink"

"Alright then mum I'll go down to the shop we need some bread and milk"

"Alright John, I'll be alright you go" so Johnny leaves, walking up the path he see's the usual gang of baseball caps and hoods on the opposite side of the road Steve looks across and sees Johnny just come out of the gate and shouts

"Eh copper is your mum missing Danny" and they all start laughing Johnny just carries on walking up the road but with the window open Jean heard what they said and she just starts crying and saying

"Why oh why should this have happened to me what have I done wrong"

The gang, with Steve being the mouth chanting at Johnny as he walks along! people that are on the same side as the gang cross over to the side Johnny is on to stay out of the way of the hoodies at the time a police car with Pc Storey and Pc Hartley is almost level with what is happening Adam Storey jumps out of the car and shouts

"You clear off or I'll run you in for disturbing the piece and harassment" they all run off just shouting! Paul Hartley gets out of the car and says

"Hi Johnny everything alright"

"It is now Paul" Adam comes across also and says

"What was that all about Johnny"

"It's what you call piss taking chanting about my mother and about what happened and I can't do a thing about it"

"We could go pick 'em up for harassment" said Paul

"What for so they can get a slap on the wrist and let out again"

"Don't bother Paul you never know they might get struck by lightening one day" Adam says

"Yea anyway we'll see you Johnny"

"Ok lads" Johnny replies going on his way.

Down at the derelict site there's Danny with Pete Lawson Gerry Armstrong and a few more kids drinking cans of Larger Pete says

"What's been happening with the law and everything Danny"?

"Come over here Pete" says Danny, they stroll across to a pillar post both with a can having a drink

"Look Pete don't breath a word you know it was a hot day the other day when it happened I got Jean in the house and she was wiping herself down wiping the sweat from her neck and tits and it just happened I held her tits and gave her a kiss and then gave her a good shag I'll tell you what Pete best fuck I've ever had pity she had to tell anybody I'd have been in there regular" by this time Diane had been listening to what Danny had told Pete she was just round the other side of the pillar tears started to run down her face she then just turned away and left before anyone saw her. Walking down the road as she was crying Pete's girlfriend Jackie saw Diane

"Hiya Di what's the matter" Diane says

"Nothing I've just had a horrible day and I'm fed up I'm going home now so I'll see ya' Jackie"

"Yea ok Di" Jackie replies

"Take care Di"

"Yea I will" and they part company.

Johnny gets back home from the shop and Jean still weeping Johnny says

"What's the matter mum" Jean replies

"I'm alright John just a little tired" not been able to tell Johnny what she heard

"Ok mum I'll make a drink and make you a sandwich you must eat something mum"

"Yes alright John I'll try"

At the police station Pc Storey and Pc Hartley just reporting in the sergeant says

"Now then lads how's thing with you two" Adam says

"Alright Sarg except we've seen Johnny taking some abuse from some of the idiots about his mother and this lad Danny Laine"

"Well if there's any news" the sergeant says

"Two of the usual clowns Joe Downs and Jason Anderson got beat up last night both in hospital with busted kneecaps and a lot of cuts and bruises"

At this time Chief inspector Alan McClure had come through and says

"Right you two Adam and Paul you can go and take some particulars from the two boys in hospital to see if we can get any clues to who did

Fury

this beating! people just can't do things like that and get away with it! Adam says

"Probably somebody did it for something them two did! something to them or some part of there family" the Chief said

"Maybe, Maybe not but if that is the case people just can't take the law into there own hands that's what we are here for alright lads don't hang around"

"Yes sir" both officers answer. The chief goes and Adam and Paul looks at the sergeant! Adam just holds his hands up says nothing and leaves.

Back down at the derelict buildings where Danny and Pete are! Steve and the rest of the gang come through

"Hiya Danny"

"Hiya Steve what's going on then?" answers Danny!

"Did you hear about Joe and Jason getting beat up last night I've heard they've got busted knee caps"

"What you've just said was true says Steve! then Steve says

"We've been giving that copper Johnny Longhurst some shit as well Danny"

"Hey Pete what time is it"

"Half past three why?"

"I've got to get home for me dad to take me to the cop shop to report in at four see ya' later"

"Yea ok Danny" they all say! Danny then runs off.

The following morning at the Laines Joe having his breakfast in the kitchen when Jill walks through

"Do you want anything else love" Jill to Joe

"No thanks love I'll be going shortly I know you haven't said anything but have you been round to the Longhurst's" says Joe

"No I haven't" answers Jill

"But I know our Shaun has!! he's blaming our Danny he told me so"

"Whatever did he do that for I'll have a word with him, look Jill" Joe says

Don Fleming

"Do you think our Danny could have done what he's been accused of"
shouting
"No I don't" answers Jill
"And don't you even think about that otherwise you and I will be falling out"
"Ok love" Joe says
"I only asked"
"Well don't ask stupid things like that any way are you going to work"
Joe says
"Yes I am love give us a kiss"
Jill says "Oh clear off then Joe" Joe looking a bit upset about things says
"Ok I will" and goes out the back way. Shaun comes in from upstairs and says
"What's you and dad shouting about"
"You if you want to know going round to her house siding with her" Jill in a stern voice
"Do you mean Mrs Longhurst mam"
"You know very well who I mean Shaun so don't be clever" Jill says
"I always thought you always used to say that how good Mrs Longhurst was and how she coped with her condition and how well she managed" Shaun said
"Yes but maybe I was wrong anyway! Jill answers Shaun when do you go back to college"
"Mam why do you talk to me like that I haven't done anything wrong have I?"
Jill says
"You shouldn't have gone round to see the dirty bitch so shut up now" in a very nasty manner.

At the Longhursts Johnny says
"Mum I have to go down to the station to see chief McClure"
"Alright love I'll be fine"
"Anything you need mum"

"No" answers Jean

"I don't need anything love just take care"

"I will mum" answers Johnny

"I'll get off then"

"Alright love" answers Jean then Johnny leaves shouting

"I'll only be about an hour mum" then leaves closing the door behind him as Johnny Is leaving getting into his car Steve and some of the baseball cap gang see's! Steve says!

"Hey the coppers going out lets pay a visit on his old women"

Gerry Armstrong says

"Count me out I'm off into town"

Steve says

"What's up Gerry" Gerry says

"Nothing I have better things to do" and leaves the rest of them Steve and the gang come outside the Longhurst's gate Steve walks down the path up to the door and knocks Jean looks startled and puzzled and shouts

"Come in" as she sits in her wheel chair Steve opens the door and puts his head round and says

"Are you missing Danny Mrs Longhurst do you want me to tell him to come to you I'll tell him you want it" Jean starts screaming Steve shuts the door and runs off he says to the kids

"Come on lets go" chanting and laughing. Jean crying and swaying from side to side in her chair and shouting out

"I can't keep taking all of this" yelling out and crying

"Why are they doing this to me reaching for the phone to contact Johnny for him to come home and she falls out of her chair onto the floor at this time Pauline knocks and enters the room she see's Jean on the floor crying Pauline says

"Jean what has happened" runs over to Jean and try's lifting her up in her chair the best way she can Jean says still crying

"Pauline phone for my John to come home please, please Pauline" of which Pauline phoned the station for Johnny.

Back at the Laines! Susan comes down from the bathroom into the living room and asks

"What's the shouting about mum" Jean says

"Shaun siding with Mrs Longhurst and going round to see her"
"What's he said to them"
"I don't know" answers Jill
"Our Danny's been good to her and she's taken advantage of him what does it tell you when she gives him 20 pound" Susan said
"I don't know what to believe?"
"Don't you start as well" Jill says in a sharp voice
"I think my son has only got me on his side in this house"
"Don't say that mum we just don't really know what has happened" Jill says
"I do" in a sharp and loud manner
"Our Danny hasn't done anything wrong except being egged on by her he's admitted he's had sex with her which he shouldn't have done which I know he is very upset about it but I believe she knew what she was doing always giving our Danny money and kissing him and saying even to me that he was a good boy but our Danny has always been a good boy who was easily led maybe it was a good job this has happened he'll know now not to trust anybody that's it now Susan so shut up about it alright?"
"Yes mum ok" Susan answers
"Where is our Danny" Jill answers by saying
"Gone out, out the way and your other brother has also gone out where to I have no idea"

Johnny gets home from the station running down the path opening the door and running into the living room Jean sobbing
"Oh John I'm pleased your home this lad opened the door put his head round and started saying
"Do you want Danny to come and see you" Jean starts crying Johnny goes to put his arms round his mother and says
"what did he look like?" Jean sobbing at this time of telling Johnny
"He was a tall ginger haired boy I haven't seen him before" Johnny says
"I have I'll get him" Jean says
"Do it within the law John and tell some of your work mates"

Fury

"I will mum, I will" answers Johnny looking really annoyed.

Down at the usual corner where the most of the baseball cap boys hang around there's Danny with Pete Lawson, Jackie Webb, Harry Pearse and a few more of the gang. Jackie says to Danny
"I saw Diane yesterday running home crying she just said she was fed up and having a bad day" Danny says
"She's probably missing me" Harry laughs and says
"Yes Danny you'd be right she's missing you" Danny says
"Where did you see her?" Jackie says
"Just a few yards up the road from here" Danny looking puzzled he says
"Had she been round the derelict buildings?" Jackie says
"I don't know she did not say she could have come from anywhere" Danny says
"I'll go and see her sometime to see if she's alright"

In the meantime Johnny had been in touch with the station and spoke to Roger Dent to tell him the lad that opened Mrs Longhurst's door was the same ginger haired lad who was chanting outside the house the day before.
Roger said
"We'll find him Johnny and bring him in" in which they did and Steve was released with a caution. Johnny keeping in touch with his brother Frankie but not telling him some things so not to upset him, Jean spoke to Frankie and told him she was alright and which he was pleased about he told his mum he'll be home soon to see her in which she was pleased about.

Danny had been to see if Diane would see him but she wouldn't through her mother when Danny went round in which he was not pleased about! Steve down with the rest of the gang bragging about what happened and let off with a caution and saying
"I'll get that bitch back for trying to get me into trouble"

Down at the Fords where there is John wife Lillian brother Billy and son Jake

"Billy I don't know if you know or not Joe Downs and that kid Jason got nobbled last night with busted knee caps looking at Jake

"Bet your pleased now Jake you stopped palling around with them I reckon that Downsey got more that makes up for killing your rabbit eh' Jake" John and Lillian smiling and Jake answering

"Yes uncle Billy"

"I always say if you look for trouble you'll find it eh' pity the law don't do anything except keep letting them off easy peesey.

At the derelict buildings Pete, Harry, Gerry and the other hoodies when Steve comes in

"Hiya lads" then stop and flexes his arms

"I bet old lass Longhurst will fancy my body eh' I just heard they buried old man Jackson why don't we go down your road Harry and really piss them off and smash there windows before they come back

"Are you coming Harry" Harry says

"No what about the rest of you" Pete says

"Why don't you take some of the little kids after all they did it last time" Steve says

"Yea come on kids" so the ten and eleven year olds follow him, Steve then feeling bigger like the leader of the gang then saying

"Come on nobody will bother you whilst I'm with you" all of them going walking towards the Jackson's picking up stones on their way down Steve says

"Where nearly there get ready" almost outside the Jackson's Steve says

"Let them go at the windows" at the same time Penny with her boyfriend Paul just coming back home Penny says

"Look Paul them kids breaking our windows again"

"I see Penny don't shout I'll get that big ginger haired bastard" Paul starts running on the opposite side of the road then across towards Steve as he nears! Paul jumps on Steve's back at the same time smacking him in the face they both land on the floor with Paul on top of Steve all of the little kids start running away Paul on top hitting Steve in the face and says

Fury

"Now then ginger ballocks how do you like that" Paul smacking Steve, Steve starts bleeding from the nose and mouth Penny then comes up and says

"That's it Paul" Paul gets up and lifts Steve up with his hair and says

"The next time you or any of your little shit heads come round here anymore or even if I see you walking in the area I'll break your fucking neck" Steve is in such a state doesn't answer then Paul shoves him and says

"Fuck off" Penny then shouts

"Paul what about the windows we'll phone the police" Paul says

"Ok well just tell them who it was and a description"

"Alright Paul but its going to upset my mum"

"Not as much when I tell her what I did to the arse hole lets find something to put up at the windows until we get them repaired" at the same time a neighbour shouts across at Paul and says

"Well done lad he got what he deserved and if you want me as a witness as you only hit him in self defence come across and let me know" Paul says

"Thanks a lot" he turns and goes into the house another man comes out and says to the other man

"I saw what happened as well that lad did the right thing its about time someone sticks up against these louts"

The following day at the police station Pc Dent sees the Sergeant

"Sarg I've got two statements from Joe Downs and Jason Anderson and both say they can't recognise the two that beat them up"

"Alright" Roger answers the Sergeant

"I'll pass them on"

At the Longhurst's Johnny bringing his mum something to eat and drink through and puts it on her table Jean says

"I don't fancy anything to eat John" Johnny replies saying

"You have to eat something mum you haven't had anything to eat in days you'll make yourself ill mum" Jean says at the same time starts crying

"I don't want anything I can't eat"

"Oh mum don't cry" Johnny then puts his arm around Jean

"Oh come on mum don't cry and upset yourself" then Pauline knocks and comes in

"Hello Jean, Johnny, ah' what's the matter Jean" Jean answers

"I can't eat, I don't want anything to eat"

"Here now" Pauline says

"Let me give you a cuddle just have a little drink of your tea Jean and I'll have one with you alright Johnny"

"I'll have a cuppa with you mum" Jean stops crying a little but tears running down her face Johnny says

"Mum I will have to go to the station I'll only be about an hour and I'll be back will you want me to do any shopping or get anything at all for you I thought I would go while Pauline's with you"

"Alright John" Jean answers

"I don't need anything love you do what you have to do I'll be alright now" Pauline comes back through with a cup of tea and some biscuits

"Well now I've got my cup of tea Jean and I've brought some biscuits through so we can dunk them in our tea is that alright"

"Yes it is Pauline" answers Jean Johnny explains to Pauline he has to go to the station and he'll be about an hour Pauline says

"Don't worry Johnny I can stay an hour with your mum can't I Jean?"

"Yes you can", answers Jean and Johnny leaves after kissing his mum and saying

"I love you mum" Jean answers

"I love you to John"

"See you later Pauline so behave yourself while I come back" both answering

"We will" John leaves and Pauline says

"Right Jean we'll dunk our biscuits now" Jean then gets a biscuit and dunks it in her tea

Fury

"Like that Pauline" both have a little giggle and Pauline then gets a biscuit and dunks it in her tea, and says

"Yes just like that"

Outside seeing Johnny leaving his home there is Steve with a badly bruised face a thick top lip and looking like a black eye coming up! along with Harry and Gerry, Steve says

"Look that coppers going out I'll put the shit's up his mother" Gerry says

"I shouldn't there's the cleaner there Pauline Trent she'll identify us all so not for me"

"Not for me as well" answers Harry

"Ok I'll do it myself I'm not scared" Steve says! Harry and Gerry says

"Well let us get well away" they then leave walking well away. Steve starts crossing the road and sees Danny

"Where ya' going Danny?" in reply Danny says

"I'm going home what are you doing Steve?"

"I'm going to give that crippled cow that's got you into trouble some shit" Danny then says

"Go on then Steve" at the time Danny's brother Shaun not too far away from them Steve runs down Jeans path up to the door, bangs on it quite loud and kicks it then shouts

"Danny don't want you anymore bitch! Will anybody do for 'ya" at the time Shaun says to Danny

"You've encouraged him to do that", Danny says

"No I haven't"

"No says Shaun! but you didn't stop him did you?" Danny then says to Shaun

"Go Ballocks!" Pauline comes running out of the house, sees Steve going out of the gate and shouts

"I recognise you, you piece of garbage" Steve then turns and says

"I haven't done anything I was just walking by" Shaun then shouts to Pauline

"It was him alright Pauline I saw everything" Steve then runs away while inside Jean is going hysterical, crying and rocking her head

Pauline enters back into the house to go and console Jean! holding her tight Jean says

"I can't keep taking this abuse and name calling, I can't!, can't!, I can't!" Pauline doesn't answer Jean just holds Pauline tight. Jean then says to Pauline

"Will you go and get my head ache tablets from the top cupboard in the kitchen, Pauline"

"Right" answers Pauline!

"I'll get the chair to stand on" while Pauline's doing that Jean has a note pad and pen, she starts trying to write a note for Johnny saying

"Please forgive me John, but I can't carry on anymore, I love you and Frankie very much and at least I'll be going somewhere where I don't have to worry and no-one can hurt me again, I hope I will be with your dad once again I love you both throughout time always your mum. When Pauline comes back in the room she says

"It's a full bottle Jean do you want me to take a couple of tablets out and put the rest back?"

"No it'll be alright just leave it with my other bottles our John will see to them when he comes back home" Pauline says

"Ah! have you been writing?"

"Yes I have" answers Jean

"Just a few lines to our Frankie" Pauline says

"Here you are then Jean your head-ache pills and your bottled water"

"Thank you Pauline you are kind!"

"Oh that's no problem at all Jean" Pauline then says

"I'll do a bit of dusting and clean the bathroom up upstairs"

"Alright Pauline" Jean answers

"Will you be alright Jean? And if you need me just shout and I'll be down"

"All right, Pauline" Pauline then toddles upstairs to do her cleaning when Pauline goes. Jean then takes all of her tablets from all of the bottles and empties them onto her table that she has next to her chair. She then starts taking all of her tablets with the water at the same time she is reading what she has written and starts crying and saying quietly

Fury

"I love you both" continuing to take her pills she writes another small note this time to Pauline saying

"I am sorry Pauline having to do what I am going to do and with you my very good friend finding me I know it's going to be a shock of which I am deeply sorry but I can't live like this! sorry Pauline love Jean" then Jean starts taking the rest of all of her tablets with the remaining water she has.

Back at the Laines Shaun goes into the house sees his mother Jill with Danny and says to his mother

"Do you know what he's done" pointing at Danny Jill says in a stern voice

"and who's he, he is your brother, he has told me he tried to stop this lad from messing around near the Longhurst's"

"Is that what he told you" answers Shaun

"Well I was there mum and he didn't do anything except encourage this Steve Shit to go and boot on Mrs Longhurst's door with abuse and yelling"

"No I didn't why are you telling lies about me Shaun, I know you've always been jealous of me but you shouldn't tell lies about me" Jill then shouts at Shaun and says

"No you shouldn't should you?"

"Mother he is a big liar"

"Shut your mouth Shaun either go out or go upstairs" Shaun looks across at Danny where Danny is giving a little smile at him.

"Yea ok mum I'll go to my room and do some studying or something" then leaves.

Back at Jean Longhurst's Pauline just coming down the stairs shouts

"I'm coming Jean, I'll put the kettle on" on entering the room she sees Jean slumped in her chair she says

"Jean are you alright" walking across, she then sees there's something terribly wrong.

"Oh no" she says! then immediately phones 999 for an ambulance and then phones for Johnny at the police station saying to the desk Sergeant

"Johnny must come home immediately" saying she believes Mrs Longhurst's is in a serious position. Straight away word gets to Johnny and he leaves immediately with Ivor Jones in front of him in a police car with siren and flashing blue lights they get there just in front of the ambulance, Johnny runs in, with Pauline holding Jean and at the same time Pauline is crying she says to Johnny

"Your mums still breathing Johnny" when two paramedics came in one of the paramedics says

"Can anyone say what has happened" Pauline says

"When I came down stairs Jean was just slumped in her chair" Johnny looked at her bottles of pills not as neat as usual and looks he says

"She's taken all of her pills" the paramedics say

"Come on we'll have to get her to the hospital without any delay" Johnny says

"Let me help you" one paramedic says

"Ok sir" then says to the other paramedic

"Go and get In touch with emergency at the hospital to let them know what we have so they can have things ready" the paramedic goes to the ambulance to contact the hospital as Johnny is helping to get his mother to the ambulance Pauline sees the note that Jean has left for her she reads it and starts crying saying

"Oh Jean" people outside watching the ambulance as it leaves Johnny goes back to the house Ivor shouts

"I'll wait for you Johnny" Johnny enters the house sees Pauline crying come on Pauline I'll lock the house up and when I get back home I'll give you a ring to let you know how things are"

"Alright Johnny" and Pauline picking the other letter up and saying

"I think this is for you" Pauline giving Johnny the letter Jean had wrote to him. At this time Ivor ran in and shouts

"Johnny are you leaving?" Johnny puts the letter in his pocket then turned and said

"Yes Ivor get me there quick I'll just lock the door" they then leave heading for the hospital rushing away very fast as Pauline is walking away some of the neighbours asked what had happened Pauline just says

" I think Mrs Longhurst has had a heart attack". At the time Susan Laine is walking home. Susan asked one of the neighbours what had happened one neighbour answers by saying

"Mrs Longhurst has been taken to hospital by the ambulance it must be something bad they wanted to be away very fast and Johnny has just left with a police escort" Susan looked surprised and shocked then carried on walking along.

At the hospital the emergency staff gave Jean a stomach pump and tried to bring her round Johnny said to Ivor

"Stay here a minute Ivor I have to contact our Frankie to let him know what has happened Johnny goes to an area to use his mobile phone he gets in touch and speaks to one of the foreman for him to let Frankie know what had happened to his mum.

Then at the oil rig the foreman goes to see Frankie and shouts "Frankie" Frankie turns and says

"Yes what's up boss" his foreman says

"I've been in touch for a chopper for you to be picked up"

"Why" Frankie says

"Your brother Johnny has phoned to tell us to tell you your mother has been rushed into hospital and he wants you to come home it's urgent" Frankie says

"Ok I'm on my way" the foreman sees Frankie before he leaves and says

"Give us a ring when everything is alright"

"Will do Peter" Frankie says

"And thanks for your help" Peter says

"That's what where here for to help each other Frankie I hope things work out alright for you all" Frankie then gets into the helicopter and takes off.

Johnny goes back to Ivor and says
"Has anybody been out yet Ivor?"
"No Johnny"

Back at the Laines Susan walks in

"Hiya mum" she says

Hello love" Jill answers

"Mrs Longhurst has been rushed into hospital says with a heart attack" Susan says, Jill then answers by saying

"Well nothing to do with us is it?" Danny says

"Mum I'm just going out for an hour and I'll be back for dad"

"Al right son" she puts her arm around Danny and gives him a kiss.

At the hospital a doctor goes to Johnny he says

"Your mother is in a side room she is still unconscious we will be keeping a close look at her until she regains consciousness, if you would like to go into her you may do"

"Thank you doctor" Johnny answers and goes in to his mother. Jean laid wired up but looking peaceful Johnny pulls a chair up to his mothers bedside and holds her hand looking at her and says

"Come on mum please wake up, please" Johnny starts shedding a few tears

"I love you mum please wake up" When he holds his mums hand close to his cheek.

Down at the corner there's Danny, Gerry, Harry, Pete Lawson and the rest of the shit heads Danny says

"Mrs Longhurst had an heart attack and is in hospital" Gerry then answers and says

"Hey Danny you must of give her too much of your body" and they all start laughing. Steve then walks up! Danny says!

"What's happened to your face Steve run into a fucking wall?"

"No" Steve answers! I thought you noticed it before!

"A Gang of kids got me down near the Jackson's! and can you have a word with your brother Danny he's going to tell the cops I banged on that bitches door he told that cleaning women who goes there that it was me" Danny says

"Why don't you tell him yourself were not talking, at this time Ivor is just coming to the crowd of the yobs and sees Steve he pulls up and gets out, walks up to Steve and says!

"Do you want to come with me to the station or would you like me to send for a police van, Steve looking shocked and says

"What for I haven't done anything wrong"

"In that case" Ivor says!

"You won't mind coming with me then! don't say no because you will only make things worse for yourself" Steve looking clever says

"I'll come to the cop shop it don't scare me" none of the rest of the gang said anything, just stood and listening Steve goes to Ivors car and gets in Ivor then drives away.

Back at the hospital Johnny sitting by his mothers side a nurse comes in to ask Johnny if he would like a cup of tea! he said

"Thank you very much that's very kind of you" the nurse says

"I'll send you one through, no problem" Johnny then goes into his pocket and then takes the letter out that his mother wrote when a lady comes in with a cup of tea for Johnny

"Thank you" He says then opens the letter it reads

"To my beloved sons Johnny and Frankie please forgive me for what I am about to do but I can't carry on anymore with what has happened and with what is happening I love you both very much" while Johnny is reading the letter tears are streaming down his face Johnny reading on "And at least I'll be going somewhere where no-one can hurt me no-more I hope I'll be with your dad once again I love you both throughout time I always will your mother! of course Johnny starts crying even more holding his mums hand again kneeling at the side of her bed, crying

"Oh mother why!, why! Oh don't let her die lord please help her lord, I don't want you to die mum please hear me mum don't leave me, please! Wake up, please come back to me, please" Johnny holding and kissing his mothers hand and crying very much so.

When down at the station Steve is being lectured by Inspector Hardy saying

"If you keep annoying people you'll be in serious trouble like an ASBO slapped on ya' but looking at the lad it looks like you've been annoying somebody who's had enough of ya', what I have said to you don't forget, this is your last caution" Steve says!

"But I haven't done anything wrong it's some people trying to get me into trouble" looking at Inspector Hardy and looking very pitiful I just seem to be in the wrong place at the wrong time I can't say anymore than that" the inspector then says

"This is still your last caution so make sure your in the right place in future alright lad" Steve then says

"Yes sir I will! thank you sir" Steve then leaves. Ivor looks at the inspector and says

"His a lying little toad sir and I know it"

"Maybe so Ivor" the inspector says

"But we can't keep locking little toe rags up send them to courts so that the courts can give them a caution, but costing the tax payer money we can't do anymore than what is laid out for us to do by our superiors" Ivor then says

"Do you know sir where the best law and order in the world but only for criminals" Ivor then leaves and says

"Good night sir"

Later at the hospital Frankie after finding out where his mother is! he walks and goes into the side room entering to see his brother Johnny sat at the side of the bed crying and his mother still unconscious Johnny stands up looking at his brother putting his arms around him crying and saying

"Mum is in a bad situation Frankie" Frankie then goes over to his mum, takes her hand looks at her then kisses her on the forehead saying

"Come on mum me and our Johnny's here to see you then we want to take you home remember you and our Johnny will be coming soon on holiday to me so we want you to get fit again come on mum" but Jean is still laying still with no movement in any part of her body Frankie says to Johnny

"What's brought all this on then Johnny" Johnny then says

"Lets go outside the room and go to the waiting area and I will have to tell you everything that has happened mum didn't want to worry you Frankie that's why I didn't contact you straight away that's what mum wanted Frankie" Johnny and Frankie sat down so then Johnny starts telling Frankie what had happened with Danny and the rape of there mother after Johnny had told everything to Frankie, Frankie saying nothing at first just looking very annoyed then says

"What's happened to the bastard?" Johnny says

"The police have taken over and he is on an electric tag until his appearance in court on the charge of rape"

"Then what Johnny" Frankie asks

"I bet he's denying it! And blaming mother he seems that fucking type come on Johnny has he confessed to it" Johnny answers and says

"No"

"But yet our mother is in this position and could die" Frankie says, Johnny then answers and says

"Mother wrote a letter to both of us Frankie I've read it" then Johnny starts crying he handed the letter to Frankie, Frankie taking the letter to read afterwards Frankie says to Johnny

"I'll kill the lanky bastard" Johnny says

"Please stay calm Frankie for mothers sake"

"Ok" Frankie answers

"I'll just use the phone and call my boss" Johnny then goes back and sees his mother. At the phone Frankie contacts his foreman

"Hello Peter Frankie here"

"Hello Frankie how is things?" Frankie says

"Not good my mother's unconscious so I don't know how long I will be here"

"That's alright Frankie" Peter says

"Take as long as it takes"

"Thanks a lot Peter I'll be in touch" Frankie and Peter then say there goodbyes Frankie then goes to his brother and mother.

The following day down at the derelict buildings Danny and Pete and the rest of the baseball caps and hoodies, drinking cans of booze Steve rolls up and says

"Hiya men got a caution from the boys In blue what a laugh the silly bastards can't do anything to me" Then Steve says

"Anybody know how the bitch is so I can give her some more shit eh' Danny?" Danny says

"Don't bring me into it I'm in enough trouble by helping people, how many people at my age would take old invalid people out and run about going to the shops and running about after them when Diane is just behind a stanchion. Walks out and says

"Only a person like you Danny who gets what he can get from people who are vulnerable or frightened of you! well I am not and you are a filthy thieving rotten bastard who has ruined a very nice lady so you could satisfy yourself only yourself Danny! I hope one day you get what you really deserve" Danny says

"Eh Diane I haven't done anything except being worked up by Mrs Longhurst I regret what happened but it was not all my fault" Diane says

"You're a fucking liar I heard you telling Pete your exploits with Mrs Longhurst and you!, you, you bastard raped her" Diane then turned away to walk away Danny says

"And where are you going now?" Diane says

"Out of your fucking way I never want to see you again so don't come round anywhere near our house otherwise the right people will find out the truth what you really did" Danny says

"Are you trying to threaten me Diane?" Diane replies and says

"No Danny it's a promise" when Steve joins in and says

"Smack her one Danny and put her straight" Diane then says to Steve

"Don't ask somebody to do something that you can't do yourself you arsehole you come and do it and I'll show you what I can do" Steve then says

"I don't hit girlies" Diane then says

"But you'd like watching somebody else do it, your pathetic what a He man you are, more like a gay boy" Steve says

"Eh Danny tell her" Danny says

"What for you talk a load of shit".

Back at the hospital Johnny and Frankie just having a stroll around when a nurse comes up and says

"Can you go to your mother" Frankie says

"Yea we will come on Johnny" entering the room there mother is in, the doctor and nurse also, the doctor turns and says

"Your mother has died without regaining consciousness" Johnny says

"No mum come back" he goes and gets his mothers hand and crying Frankie seems numbed by things with his eyes watering he then also starts crying he goes over and puts his arms round Johnny he also holds his mums hand after a while Johnny and Frankie leave Frankie with his arms around his brother walking to Frankie's hired car, Johnny says

"I'll have to go in my car Frankie I came in it yesterday"

"Ok" Frankie says

"Lets head for home now then Johnny" Johnny says

"I'll just contact the station to tell them what's happened and I'll be away from work for a while"

"Ok Johnny do what you have to do" Johnny contacts the station then heads home.

The desk Sergeant at the station informs Inspector Hardy straight away and in walks Ivor Jones the Sergeant tells Ivor that Mrs Longhurst has passed away, Ivor says

"That piece a shit Laine will get away with the rape now and along with helping Jean die what can I say except sadness for Johnny and his brother".

Frankie and Johnny getting back home out of the cars walking towards the front gate as Shaun Laine is walking up Shaun shouts

"Hiya Johnny how's your mum" Johnny turns and says

"Tell your brother our mother has just died" Shaun looks shocked and says

"I'm ever so sorry Johnny" Johnny along with Frankie say nothing else, except walk down the path and into the house, Shaun runs home running down the road into the gate and down the path and in through the front door Shouting

"mum, dad" Joe Laine walks through into the room followed by Jill and Susan Joe says

"What's the matter son?" Shaun says

"Mrs Longhurst has just died" Jill says

"How do you know that?" Shaun says

"I've just seen Johnny and Frankie coming home from the hospital and Johnny told me" everything goes quiet in the Laine household probably nobody not knowing what to say, except just look at each other. A few minutes pass and Danny walks in the back door through the kitchen and into the room, sees everybody very quiet he says

"What's the matter with everybody?" Jill says

"We just heard Mrs Longhurst has died"

"Who says so" Danny says! Shaun then replies

"Johnny Longhurst just back from the hospital with his brother told me he wanted me to tell you Danny" Danny says

"Why tell me I didn't do anything for her to die" Shaun says

"Didn't you Danny?" Joe then says

"That's it Shaun we can't do anything about anything now so don't lets argue amongst ourselves"

As almost a week goes by the day of Mrs Longhurst's funeral people out in the street neighbours and friends including Jill Laine, standing with Shaun and Susan, Frankie with his arms around Johnny who was crying Frankie looking strong also very bitter with what's happened. Family and friends getting into the funeral cars Pauline walks up behind Jill and says

"You know Jill I think you should know Jean committed suicide because she couldn't cope with the abuse she was getting from your Danny's friends and what had happened"

"You can't say that" answers Jill

"She died of a heart attack" Pauline says

"No she never I'll let you read the note she left me while I was upstairs cleaning she took all her tablets and then said she was sorry that I would have to find her that's what kind of person she was kind and honest" Jill read the note and handed it back to Pauline saying nothing and walking away Shaun and Susan following. The entourage heading up the road to the church.

Jill goes home and sees Joe she cries as soon as she sees him, Joe says

"Alright love alright" Jill says

"Joe Jean committed suicide she wrote a note for Pauline, she took every tablet she had" at this time Danny walked in

"What's up with everybody why are you crying mum" Shaun says

Fury

"Mrs Longhurst committed suicide because she could not live with what had happened and your stupid mates including that idiot Steve what ever his name is by shouting abuse and banging on her door when Mrs Longhurst was by her self, all a set of brave bastards" Joe then says

"Don't swear Shaun"

"Ok dad" Danny replies

"Well you can't blame me for that I didn't tell them to do whatever they did"

"I never said you did Danny but you never stopped it"

"Oh I'm going out again" but Joe replied

"No you aren't Danny you stay here alright"

"Yes ok dad" Danny answers.

After the funeral which was attended by a lot of people including family friends including Ivor Jones and Inspector Hardy from the police Pauline and even Diane ex girlfriend of Danny's! after leaving Pauline was walking with Diane, Diane says to Pauline

"Aren't you Mrs Longhurst's cleaner" Pauline answers saying

"Yes" Diane then says

"I used to go out with Danny Laine but I have nothing to do with him now because I know he did rape Mrs Longhurst I heard him talking about it with a friend of his Pete Lawson he was telling Pete how he had her" Diane then a little weepy Pauline says

"Shouldn't you tell the police" Diane says

"Why they'll both deny that anything was said I know how they work Danny would say I was only trying to get him into trouble because we no longer go out with each other, but I just had to tell someone" Pauline says

"You poor girl".

Back at the Longhurst's Johnny and Frankie sat down talking Johnny saying

"How could all this happen Frankie"

"I don't know Johnny, we'll probably never know! all I do know is that mum wouldn't of egged him on that's for sure, I wonder what the Laine's will be thinking when they find out mum committed suicide when you think mum and Jill were good friends she never even tried to come round and see mum only the young lad Shaun a different lad all together compared

to all the other bastards" says Frankie, Johnny then says
"When will you have to go back Frankie" Frankie answered and says
"I'll go back in another couple of days I'll let Peter know"

A couple of days later Frankie saying his good-bye to Johnny and saying he'll be back after a couple of weeks Johnny saying
"I'll get everything sorted here Frankie" Frankie and Johnny walking out to the front gate then Frankie getting into his car he waves and leaves! Johnny turns to go back into the house when he sees Danny walking along with Pete Lawson when Danny sees Johnny looking he turns back and says to Pete
"Come back this way Pete" Pete realizing why and turns back Johnny shouts
"you do know Danny you've killed my mother" Danny and Pete just carried on walking only faster! Frankie on his way back up to Scotland talking out loud with tears in his eyes with hatred!
"That bastard Danny Laine doing this to my mother but he won't get away with it he thinks he will now she's gone but the fucking arse hole with my mother killing herself what that bastard did" he will pay in full.

Down at the Laines Joe talking to Jill
"I think I should find out what is going to happen about our Danny and this electric tag now Mrs Longhurst is dead! will he be going to court"
"I can't see that! no it's our Danny's word against who! unless he says he raped her there is no case" Jill says
"You see to things Joe I can't"
"What's the matter Jill we have to clear all this up for our Danny's sake"
"I know Joe" answers Jill

Fury

"Or do you think there is something more that we don't know about"

"And are you still thinking that our Danny is guilty of what happened round at the Longhurst's" replies Joe

"No! I don't know" answers Jill, Joe then says

"Jill this is your son where talking about if he hasn't got us to help him who has he got?" Danny then walks in and doesn't say anything Joe turns and says

"Are you alright son?" Danny answers saying

"Yea alright thanks dad I'm just going upstairs"

"All right lad" Joe replies Jill and Joe just looking at each other.

The following day Danny is down at the Derelict place talking to Pete, Gerry, Steve and Harry, Danny saying!

"Mrs Longhurst committed suicide" Steve answers!

"She must have missed ya' Danny" Pete then says

"Why don't you shut your fucking mouth" looking at Steve

"What's up with you I'm only having a bit of fun".

At the police station Inspector Hardy speaking to Ivor Jones

"I've had a call from Mr Laine wanting to know what our intention of what's going to happen now that Mrs Longhurst is dead I have spoken to the chief and it looks like young Laine will be coming in to have the tag taken off and it looks very much like their will be no case although admitted having sex! so it was Mrs Longhurst encouragement that it happened" Ivor says!

"Yes sir but we know different don't we sir".

So the following day, Danny gets his tag taken off looking that he has got away with things so he can carry on doing what ever he want's again.

On that same night Danny going home walking up the back alley to his home walking towards him a figure of a man as he gets closer Danny wondering suspiciously and looking all the time at the oncoming figure when he sees who it is its Frankie Longhurst but before Danny could get away Frankie grabbed him and hit him face first then fisted him in the chest Danny went down and out like a falling tree Frankie looking about to see if there is anybody about he then lifts Danny up and carries him to his car not far away he opens the boot of his car and puts Danny inside Frankie always looking to see if there is anybody about, luckily not, he then gets into the car and drives away, he goes well out of the way and stops he goes and opens the boot Danny still out cold Frankie then puts tape around his ankles then his hands and finally round his mouth he gets back into the car and carries on.

Back at the Laines Jill says
"It's getting very late Joe I wonder where our Danny is"
"It's only half past ten love now he's had the tag off he's probably with his girlfriend or with somebody talking and forgetting the time"
"Maybe so Joe" answers Jill.

Later Frankie arriving where he has his boat moored in the early hours not a soul in sight which is good and everything seems to be going to plan for him, he gets out of his car and opens the boot where Danny is, Danny now with his eyes open he looks up at Frankie not taking any notice Frankie picks Danny up and out of the boot walking to his boat he takes Danny on board and down into the engine room he then puts him down Danny looks a bit distraught and worried about what Frankie is going to do, Frankie then says
"Right Danny boy I am going to take the tape off that's round your mouth, but the first time you shout loud it goes back on do you understand" Danny answers by bowing his head up and down Frankie then removes the tape, Danny then says
"What are you going to do Frankie" Frankie says
"Well first of all you raped my mother I knew my mother and she would not have done what you said happened you say one lie to me and you will regret deeply so think about it and you better tell the truth remember there is only the two of us here nobody else, you did rape my mother and I want to know why" Danny starts crying and says
"I couldn't help myself I just wanted to love her I've always loved your mum Frankie and I didn't want her to die" Frankie says
"You even stole twenty pounds from her and said she paid you that! you lied all arse ends up didn't you" Danny looking down at the floor and said nothing but still crying
"You also know" Frankie says

"Why she killed herself don't you" Danny says
"No I don't I don't know"
"Well besides what you did to her to humiliate her! answers Frankie! she had to take a lot of shit from the shitheads you knock around with and she couldn't take anymore so she committed suicide and took away everything that was anything to me so not only did you rape her you also caused her death so you are as guilty as sin and that you would get away with it! well I'm going to show you what I have for you, a concrete block with a steel ring in bedded in the concrete with a chain and very thick padlock and I'm going to take you on a trip in the boat fishing but in the mean time" Frankie gags Danny again chains his legs with the chain going through the steel ring in bedded in the concrete

"See you in the morning Danny boy" Frankie then leaves and locks everything up.

Back at the Laine's its now six o clock in the morning Jill looking a bit upset and says

"Joe I wonder where our Danny is he's never stayed out all night before"

"I've no idea I'll send our Shaun out to see if he can find him" Joe replies

"But I'll have to go to work soon love phone me up at work when he gets home".

Back at Frankie's boat Frankie going on board when one of the locals sees Frankie and shouts

"Frankie" in a Scottish accent the man says

"Are you out today on your boat Frankie" Frankie replies and says

"I'm going out for a spot of fishing and a bit of piece and quiet"

"I with the upset you've had Frankie laddie look after yourself and have a pleasant day out"

"I hope so" Frankie says

"See you maybe when I get back"

"I hope so Frankie with a lovely piece of Haddock"

"Ok" Frankie says

"See you later"

Don Fleming

"I see ya' later laddie" Frankie goes down to the engine room where Danny is laid looking up Frankie looking down at him and saying

"Right o Danny boy where going fishing" Frankie then goes up to the bridge starts up the engine then goes and takes the mooring ropes off he then jumps back aboard and leaves for the open sea.

Back at the Laines, Jill goes upstairs into Danny's bedroom to have a look around in case there maybe some clue or anything! wondering why Danny has not come home she looks in the draw's besides looking at the top of the wardrobe and in the bottom draw under some newspapers Jill comes across a box with gold sovereigns inside another box with lots of money inside Jill looks at the newspaper that is inside the draw saying about the rape of Mrs Longhurst but no name of Danny through legal reasons she starts crying Susan then comes through and says

"What's the matter mum?" Jill weeping looking at the newspaper and saying

"I bet our Danny's run away with all the trouble that's happened" Susan says

"Our Shaun's been out to find out where he could be or could have gone and everybody who he spoke to just said

"the last time they saw him was about eleven o' clock last night and they thought he was going home! what's all that mum that you have?" Jill says

"I've taken these boxes out of our Danny's draw I don't know how he could have got all this money and gold sovereigns I just don't know what's happening anymore" Susan says

"What are you going to do mum?"

"I don't know" Jill replies

"I'll wait until your dad gets home and hope our Danny hasn't run away then he can explain everything"

Frankie well out at sea he anchors up then he has his fishing rod over the side with the rod well held down with some weights holding the rod, he then goes down to Danny, unlocks the padlock

"Look Danny boy what I have for you some goggles and a divers air tank and I have the same for myself where going into the sea" Frankie

Fury

gets the concrete and chain to the deck then carries Danny up chains him back up to the concrete and steel ring, puts Danny's goggles on and air tank pulls the tape from his mouth and puts in the mouth piece!! Frankie then put's his goggles and air tank on along with flippers he drags the concrete with Danny attached to the side Danny starts struggling to no avail Frankie hangs the concrete over board! out into the distance nothing in site only a few gulls before Frankie puts his mouthpiece in he looks and says to Danny

"You'll have half an hour of air to breath to think about what you have done, think about everything you have done"

"I'll be coming down part way with you I'd like to come all the way but its far too deep here" he then shoves Danny overboard then follows him at the same time he holds Danny from going down to fast and goes with him until Frankie waves bye bye to him Danny shaking about but its not going to do him any good he's going down with terrifying looks! Frankie heads back to the boat getting on board taking his things off putting them away then goes down to the engine room, tidy all up so there is no incriminating evidence that Danny has been aboard also cleaning and washing the deck down when he sees his fishing rod moving about and he reels it in Frankie then sees he has caught a fish he just looks and says

"Well blow me" with Danny in total fear at the bottom of the sea! Frankie starts the engines and ups the anchor and moves elsewhere as he is steering the launch he is thinking out loud to himself

"I just hope he's fearful like my mother was my mother knew when she was going to die when she took all of her pills he'll know when he is as well when the oxygen runs out".

Back at the Laine's Joe coming home from work, as soon as Joe gets in Jill tells him what she has found in Danny's bedroom Jill and Joe go upstairs and Joe sees for himself what's there"

"Where's all this money come from I wonder" Joe says

"And these gold sovereigns" Joe then says

"Hey! wasn't there gold sovereigns took from that old lady that was beat up and robbed a while ago" Jill says

"I don't know Joe! what has our Danny been doing" Joe then says

"What do we do, do we go to the police tell them what we have found here and tell them our Danny is missing, what shall we do" Jill says

"It was only last night Danny didn't come home lets wait".

At the station Chief Super Alan McClure and Inspector John Hardy in the Inspector's office

"Well John" the chief says

"we have had so many complaints about certain yobs it could be that asbo orders will be taken out on them and a curfew order that's the only thing that can be done"

"Great isn't it Sir, what kind of punishment is that these arseholes wont be bothered they'll just carry on as normal the only way for these things is corporal punishment and public floggings does anybody think that, that would stop what they do, I think national service to be brought back and make shit heads into men and to respect others I don't believe the prisons will be full anymore! Them that are full that even ardent criminals get away with things bring hanging back for proven murderers things need to be done soon! because if not! people that suffer today from these things but can't be named for legal reasons these idiots have worse to come themselves when they get older and have family's of there own if they reach old age things will certainly get worse but there'll always be a handful of do-gooders that haven't felt the wrath of these people they want to protect! I think they would have a different opinion if anything happened to themselves or there own family"

"I know what your saying John" answers the chief

"But we can only carry on and do what the law at the moment tell us to do"

"Yes I know sir that's why in a week or so I'll be out of the force"

"I do know sir that there is more than me up and down the country that feel the same

but most will carry on being policemen because it's a job with pay and a living but what about people in the country that have to live in fear from our own home grown arse holes and according to what I've read in the newspaper these what's put on ASBO orders is a badge of honour for others to follow, a badge of honour to be an ASBO brilliant isn't it sir" the chief just looking at inspector Hardy shaking his head slightly from side to side.

Down at the corner where Danny's old mates are Pete Lawson says to Harry Pearse
"Has nobody seen Danny since the night before last" Harry answers
"No" at the same time an old boy is walking by with the aid of his walking stick when one of the gang banged a tin lid the old man jumped Harry says shouting
"Did that make you jump you silly old fart?" at the time three teenagers walking not far away from the old man, one says
"Who are you calling an old fart you bastard that's my grandad come here you Dick head then Harry starts running away then the three lads start chasing him Harry realising he was being closed down he runs into a house crying a man comes to the door Harry says
"Them three lads are trying to get me, to beat me up" the man says
"Why don't you leave him alone three big lads like you this lads only about fourteen at school" Harry says
"Yes Mr I'm only fourteen"! the lad who's grandad it was up the road says
"I'll see you sometime soon I'm bound to" they then walked away" Harry says to the man
"I was only going to the shop for an old lady who lives near me who can't get out herself" the man says
"You look a good boy I think you'll be alright now" Harry says
"Thank you Mr" and leaves.

These kind of kids are experts at lying they lie so much they nearly always use the same lines,
"Who me…I don't know what your talking about… I'm only a child at school, etc etc etc…"

The following day Danny still not home nobody's seen him so Joe Laine has to go to report it to the police, at the station he sees the desk Sergeant Paul Stretton to report that his son Danny is missing, he says

"I think my son has run away because of what has happened I have brought this money and gold sovereigns in of what we found in his bedroom we don't know where they have come from all we know he wouldn't have been able to save all that amount up and the sovereigns no idea we've never had any" the desk Sergeant Stretton says

"The sovereigns could have come from a break in and theft at the old lady Mrs Stones who was beaten up whom is still in hospital and later her bungalow was set on fire after a robbery there anyway! Mr Laine you have been very honest to have brought these in for us we'll put a missing person message out and when he returns we will find out how he came by them" Joe says

"Our Danny must have got the money and sovereigns from his so called mates"

"Maybe so sir we'll find out when Danny returns home" and as Joe is leaving the station Johnny Longhurst is just walking in, he sees Joe! Johnny and Joe just looking at each other without saying anything Sergeant Stretton sees Johnny and says

"Hiya Johnny how are you doing?"

"Ok Sarge" answers Johnny

"What's he want, Joe Laine, Paul?" the sarge says

"he came in to report his son Danny missing believed to have run away for some reason and also brought a pile of money and some gold sovereigns! he's been missing now two days" Johnny says

"He's probably nicked them the Sergeant says

"Probably Johnny but why didn't he take the money with him, with him running away" Johnny says

"Probably if and when he's picked up he would be asked where he got all the money so I should imagine he's just took enough that he thinks he'll need until he decides to come back he probably thought his parent's wouldn't find what he had and if they did they wouldn't report it and bring it to the police at least now he has made a mistake that we may get him on something now"

"What a brake I can't wait for him to be picked up well I hope for you and your family Johnny" Sergeant Stretton says.

Later that evening at the Longhurst Johnny phones Frankie up on the rig to ask how he's keeping Frankie says

"I'm ok Johnny are you?" Johnny replies

"Yea I'm feeling a lot better now I think we have something on Danny Laine now" and tells Frankie what has happened Frankie then says to Johnny

"You know Johnny sometimes justice is better outside the law" Johnny at the other end of the line looking puzzled

"What do you mean Frankie" Frankie answers by saying

"I'm just saying to you Johnny! that justice sometimes is better outside the law"

Imagining and seeing the look of fear that would be on Danny Laine's face.

The end.

The Writers Epilogue:

As it is at this moment in time, the law is on the side of the criminal

Human rights means nothing only to the guilty they use it, the only time the guilty is sorry is when they get found out

There is more crime than ever; I don't believe that crime is going down,

That we are led to believe.

Most of the criminals don't even go to jail, those that do live a life of riley.

I have never known so many windows being smashed just for the fun of it

By young kids aged from 9 yrs of age, maybe younger, and they get away it,

Usual conditional discharge, The gangs that attack people for no reason and the individuals that they do attack often receive serious injuries and in some cases they have lost their lives and that is a known fact. Then the government come out with more rubbish but good for the criminals, I read that prisoners would be let out of prison but why was they in there for in the first place. They say they could become useful citizens who for? Then the politicians that at this time were trying to have it passed that burglars would not have to go to prisons, hey good again for the criminals! Not so good for the good law biding people.

I believe that if police are not allowed to do their jobs and the judges are not allowed to sentence people for what they should receive the governing body allowing people to get away with crimes.

There would not be overcrowded prisons if hanging came back into force for murderers along with corporal punishment.

If things are to carry on the way it is! one day! I believe people's vigilantes will do the job for the innocent.

Unless the laws are changed sooner than later thing's will get worse that is also a fact.

Although the ending of this story is fictional, what kind of ending should it have been?

HE WILL BE CALLED WONDERFUL
COUNSELLOR, MIGHTY GOD,
EVERLASTING FATHER, PRINCE OF PEACE....
ISAIAH 9 : 6